The WARS of LOVE

A NOVEL

by Mark Schorer

"It's not my world, I grant, but I made it." JOSEPHINE MILES

SECOND CHANCE PRESS
RD2, Noyac Road
Sag Harbor, N.Y. 11963

PS 3537
C 597
W3
1982

BOOKS BY MARK SCHORER

A HOUSE TOO OLD

THE HERMIT PLACE

THE STATE OF MIND

WILLIAM BLAKE: THE POLITICS OF VISION

THE WARS OF LOVE

Originally published by McGraw-Hill Book Company, Inc.,
New York.
First republication 1982 by Second Chance Press,
RD2. Sag Harbor, New York

Copyright © 1954 by Mark Schorer
© 1982 by Ruth Schorer Living Trust, Ruth P. Schorer Tr. and
Trust u/w/o Mark Shorer, Page Schorer Tr.

Library of Congress Catalogue Card Number: 82-061041
International Standard Book Numbers:
(U.S.) 0-933256-34-5 (Clothbound)
0-933256-35-3 (Paperbound)

Printed in the United States of America

144356

For Eleanor and Kenneth Murdock

N. L. TERTELING LIBRARY
ALBERTSON COLLEGE OF IDAHO
CALDWELL, ID 83605

ONE

Summers in the Country, When Young

1

When we remember, at least, we are all artists. I try to remember 1924. And I know that whatever we are or profess to be in our active, present lives, magnificent or ordinary, even bestial, broken, and dull, we are by right of vanished lives, structures of memory underneath, and these are in some ways like works of art, although secret. Memory selects, distorts, organizes, and by these, evaluates; then, fixes! This is the artistic process, except for that final step beyond process which makes of the work an object capable of life and meaning outside ourselves, independent. But the operations of memory are our very selves, and are always taking independence from us. Thus our future is our past.

I begin in this unpromising way because what I have to write is founded on an exercise of memory, and memory can betray us as smilingly as a treacherous friend; I know, for I have told this story—have tried to tell this story before, and in the very telling it has somehow slipped away from me, so that it has never quite come out in the way that it should, and I am still determined that it can. And further, I begin in this way, reader, to give you that fair warning which is your right. I am, as you will see, an honest man; honesty, indeed, has been my profession: I have been paid to be honest. Being honest, I recognize at the outset that the deepest lies are those that we do not intend, those that we do not really know we have committed. Or think of it in a different way—like Joseph Conrad, when he wrote that "A meditation is always—in a white man, at least—

3

more or less an interrogative exercise." Certainly some of what
I have to write here is meditation, and unless that were in part
a matter of self-questioning, I should probably have no urgent
desire to tell it.

Yet I am not a central character. I am less important in this
story than any of the others. The others are, chiefly, three:
Daniel Ford—you know the name; his wife, Milly—you know
her face; and Freddie Grabhorn, their friend. The other
woman, the incomparable Josephine Drew, who, as the chief
witness for the State necessarily received a good deal of attention from the press and is therefore likewise known to the public, is not really a character in their story, although she is promi-
nent in mine. I am only Grant Norman, once their friend. Of
these, Dan, who was the weakest, was the best, and the center,
surely, and it is surely Dan whom I wish to vindicate.

His difficulty was that common one, the difficulty of vocabu-
lary. He had no other way of describing his act, and the way he
took was wrong, simply wrong. When, almost at the beginning
of his trial, in one of the few strong moments of his adult life,
he said, and said so tritely, "Yes, I did it. I did it because they
betrayed me; she—my wife, after all, and he—our friend";
when he said that before a crowded, gaping courtroom, he
eliminated forever the possibility of establishing in its real
terms the disastrous record. The defense attorneys, who had
some idea of the true situation but not, I think, a very clear
one, found themselves helpless in a net of clichés, and in the
end they let the clichés stand; for the truth, the real nature of
the betrayal, recited in a courtroom before that panting audience, would have given them less ground on which to rest Dan's
case. Like all human motives, which necessarily grow into ab-
stractions, honor has meaning for most of us only in its baldest,
dreariest terms, and those were the terms that Dan's lawyers
finally employed. Yet Dan's was an intricate cuckoldry!

We think in patterns, in neat and recognizable and largely factitious forms of experience, and we impose these ready-made forms on events in order that events may be comprehensible to us; and this is the particular vice of the law, of judges, attorneys, and juries, and of their fellows, the habitual spectators, those anonymous persons who haunt and color criminal trials with the crude enthusiasm of religious fanatics. These are the black and white squares by means of which temporal justice can alone be made to seem, perhaps, an order; but they have little to do with human motives or with that absolute justice that some men are satisfied to think exists in another realm, and toward which anarchy, dissatisfied, aspires in this one.

Hence it was in no way surprising that the whole thing should have been recorded in the legal annals of this state as a commonplace sex crime, the simple triangle and one sick mind, and that Dan, a really harmless though profoundly dishonored man, should have been judged for his offense in the terms of this state, appropriate to his offense as it was understood. And yet his trial explained nothing, justified nothing. If this had been the conventional triangle, the catastrophe would have been very different: for that, Dan could not have found the strength to be so drastic. It may, therefore, be worth trying to straighten out the record, not, certainly, for any legal reasons—legally, Dan's offense would have been the same, or worse because less explicable, and his motives of no importance except to that audience intent on verifying its assumption that man is both base and comprehensible—but for the human reasons. It may be possible to piece this story out so that it makes some sense on that more subtle and, psychologically, more violent level that alone can explain it.

For, to begin, these were subtle people—Milly, with her anfractuous pride, and Freddie, with his not quite simple jealousy—subtle in the way of the most profoundly immoral human beings, those who live alone in the involuted tower of willfulness; Dan, a weak man, subtle as a demonstration of the twisted forms that deterioration of the will can take. Of myself I need say nothing: the fact that, as this situation developed over the years, I had almost completely dropped out of the relationship, attests to my fundamental simplicity. But in the beginning we were all friends, and to understand—even for me to understand—what happened to our friendship and their love, it has been necessary to say as simply as possible these things.

2

At the head of one of those many lakes with Indian names in the Cherry Valley is a small town named Silverton. In winter it is buried in snow and isolated from the world; in summer it is hot, but its life enjoys an annual resurrection through the economic grace of the twenty-five or thirty families that come to occupy the large houses set on the sloping lawns above the lake. That, at any rate, was its situation in the first thirty years of this century, and I presume that today it is much the same. I have not been in Silverton for many years. In 1930 my father's house on the lake was put on the block, together with other tangible remnants of the fiasco that was his life, and after that I had no reason to return. I was nineteen years old, I had moved far away, I had to use my summers to earn money, and I had by then drifted loose from the friendship that, for almost ten years, had been my summer life.

The beginnings of that friendship, how we first came together and came first to live so deeply in one another's lives, elude me. They are lost in undifferentiated recollections of hot, insect-singing days and cooling nights, of thunderstorms over the lake and the tops of trees swaying heavily in the wind and meadow grass laid flat to the earth by rain, fragments of children's parties—sticky hands and crepe paper and grass stains on starched white linen, of children's lives when they are lost still in the giant lives of parents. Of those beginnings, nothing now coheres, but dissipates itself in memory like wisps of music or of smoke vanishing on wind. Being so near in age and our three houses standing side by side, Milly and Dan and I must always have been together, from our earliest years, yet nothing of the early years now shapes itself into event. Nothing coheres until that summer when Freddie entered, but from then on, in general outlines and in much of the detail, it is nearly all formed and clear to me.

Freddie was the outsider, a boy from the town, the son of a dentist who had many children, eight or nine. In a vague way, as summer people are of townspeople in a place like Silverton, we must have been aware of Freddie, but on a June day in 1924, he became, as it were, one of us. We were walking in a narrow, curving ravine between hills, along the dried-up gravel bed of a springtime stream. Birches grew up from us on both sides, their scarred white trunks thin and bright in the sunlight, leaves shuddering silver-green. There was a commotion of noisy birds above us somewhere, and we paused to look up through the patchwork of leaves, and then, as we stood together, three things happened in quick succession. Something whizzed through the air and up into the branches above us, there was a great fluttering in the branches and a crow plummeted to the gravel at our feet, flailing its wings, and Freddie Grabhorn came running around the curve in the hill ahead. He stopped suddenly when he saw us, stared and waited.

We stood with the dying bird between us, watching the final feeble efforts of its wings. The bird's head was bloody where a stone had hit it, and the wings spread out slowly in the sun, on the clean gravel, like a fan of jet. We were silent. The wind stirred a feather. Beside me, Dan sighed deeply.

We looked up at the boy. He flicked a slingshot against the leg of his overalls with exaggerated idleness, and his eyelids flicked. Light leaf shadows wavered on his face like a mysterious mask and, perhaps, made that round and somewhat heavy face seem more sullen than it was. Then he smiled uneasily. Milly stepped round the bird and said to him, "Let's see." He handed her his slingshot, and she turned it over in her hands. "Show me how?" she asked.

He took it from her and when he had found a small round stone that pleased him, he placed it in the oval patch of leather that hung from the forked wood, pulled back on the rubber strips, and let the pebble fly up into the trees in an easy arc. Then he handed it back to Milly. Dan and I stepped round the bird and stood beside her.

"Aim it at something," Freddie told her.

"The top of that tree," she said, and aimed, and missed. She smiled at him, as if to apologize for her incompetence, and tried again. She missed again, and tried a third time. I said, "Let's see it, Milly," and she gave it to me. Dan and I studied it.

"Haven't you ever seen a slingshot?" he asked us, and when Dan handed it back, he gave it once more to Milly. "You want it?"

"Oh!" she said with suppressed pleasure, but hesitated, her hands at her chest.

"Go ahead. I can make another." He put it in her willing hands, and then he said to Dan and me, with a quizzical smile that seemed almost to say he was testing *us*, "Want to make some?"

"Sure!" we said together.

He dug in his pocket for a large knife with brown bone clasps. He opened its largest blade, sharpened to a blue gleam. "Come on then."

We found a cluster of maple saplings that Freddie said were right, and we cut off three forked branches that he said would do, and while, under his instruction, we peeled the bark and notched the branch ends with the single knife, Milly practiced her aim. We sat in the sun on a grassy slope, and soon we began to hear her stones bouncing with light thuds off the tree trunks she was hitting.

"We need an inner tube, and some leather, like from an old, soft shoe, and some strong twine," Freddie said.

Before we started back to my father's house, where we could find these necessities, we stood around and watched Milly in the ravine. "Now I'm going to get a bird," she said, and as she looked around in the treetops, her lifted face was thin and tight with determination. We waited quietly. Freddie put one hand cautiously on her shoulder and pointed to direct her eyes. She took aim, the stone whizzed, there was a noisy fuss in a tree, birds scattered in the sky, but no bird dropped. We waited again until a number had once more assembled in the branches. Then Freddie took the slingshot, fitted in his stone, aimed with one eye wickedly closed, and let fly. A threshing about in the leaves, and then a bird dropped heavily to a slope of hill and rolled over and down a little. I felt Dan jerk in a spasm of sympathy, and "Ah!" we all said, and again, but from a distance, we watched a glossy crow stretch its wings and fold into death; and going back, and always after that, there were four of us, not three.

The summer of 1924 became a summer of constant rain.

Freddie and I were thirteen, Dan and Milly twelve. I have observed since then the fickle shiftings and alterations of all friendship among children, how a group of children, small or large as it may be, is never long equal and unanimous. Three always push out one, and cruelly; four one, then two; then presently the whole alignment of loyalties changes again. This is the normal pattern, yet it was never ours, and ours was to be the consequent loss. Freddie merged his life in ours with a hungry passion, and if he had friends in the town or a life there, he hardly told us, and we, who had no curiosity about the village, did not, I suppose, ask. Our friendship and our life were what he wanted, and he wanted them from all of us, not from only one or two. He wanted, perhaps, not us at all, but what together we represented for him: the alien, the urban, and, through village eyes, the rich. He owned a bicycle which he had earned the summer before by delivering a city newspaper up and down the lake shore, and almost every morning, as the leisurely life of the lake houses was just beginning, Freddie would have finished with his papers and appear for the day. He had had a job as caddy at the golf club, too, but now he gave that up; he told us that it took too much time.

Milly had a special, feminine respect for his country wisdom and for his array of devices, of which the slingshot and the big knife were only the first two; and she welcomed him: if he felt some hunger to be one of us, she felt some reciprocal hunger to have him. Milly's mother was dead. She had two brothers who were eight and ten years older than she, and a father, Gregory Moore. The brothers, triumphant young gods from Princeton who drove a Marmon and were perpetually in the center of those sporting and social activities which comprised adult summer life on the lake, were without interest in her, and that summer Gregory Moore almost never came to Silverton from the city, even for week ends. He was a man in his mid-forties then, with black hair turning white, and hot black eyes, and a remote speech and manner, so abstractedly gentle that gentleness was not at all the point; a romantic figure, if only because popular opinion held that for the seven years since his wife's death he had lived in that death entirely, his grief and his sense of the gross injustice that had been done him, transformed into energies fiercely concentrated on his Albany law office. He opened his summer house for his children, and let the management of it rest solely with a housekeeper, Mrs. Colby, the capable, good-natured widow who likewise managed his household in the city. Mrs. Colby was professionally tolerant of us, and we had the run of the Moore house in a way that we did not have of our more conventionally organized houses. This laxity was no doubt arranged by Gregory Moore's orders, issued perhaps from some vague feeling of penitence, since he gave Milly little besides his houses. Once Milly showed her friendship for Freddie, Mrs. Colby accepted him, too, with the same placid tolerance. In every real sense, of course, she was totally indifferent to all of us, and that did not matter—was, indeed, our advantage, except that most particularly she was indifferent to Milly. Or should I say that Milly alone needed something more than indifference from her?

And therefore Milly bound us, held us to her and held us to one another, and in Freddie, with his different motives, she found her perfect ally. I am wrong if I seem to suggest that either of them so early in life made any real calculations about friendship (although we later learned there was at least deliberateness in Freddie), but I am as sure that they both felt equally strong although different needs as I am that those early needs grew into their later, calculated, enmeshing deeds.

Milly dressed like a boy then, in dungarees or, more frequently, in shorts like ours, and a striped jersey. She insisted to Mrs. Colby that her straight blond hair be kept cut ruthlessly short, almost like a boy's, with a fringe of it always falling across her eyes, but since this was not unlike the prevailing fashion among young women, it did not seem as remarkable as it was. She had serious, gray-blue eyes, and even though her white skin turned golden tan, her face had the lean look of the underfed with, sometimes, a strange translucence. She was a small child, small-boned, shorter than most girls of eleven and twelve, and thin besides; yet physically she was inexhaustible, the most able of us, the last to rest, and of a perfect grace. She held her head high even then, and she had a kind of presence, an authority that had nothing to do with her sex. She never argued or quarreled, even then, and when the rest of us began an argument, she had a way of taking charge and shifting the ground of discussion to gain a frozen peace between us.

Do I read this back into an unwarrantable past? I think not. Listen— That summer the rain became incessant, days and nights of it together, and trees and shrubs grew with a sickening vigor, crowding the shore and the houses, defeating gardeners, and gardens turned into fecund, unflowered jungles, sable green in the rain, and, when the sun broke through, steaming with damp, cloying smells of sodden earth and mould. We spent the rainy hours in the big attic of the Moore house, an enormous area under a multishaped roof, containing among other relics that provided distraction, a spinning wheel, a series of large plaster heads of German composers, a wood-burning set, a collection of naval flags, and, most remarkable, a suit of armor. At the center, the attic was high enough to support a hoop through which we could toss baskets, and for a week we amused ourselves with an abandoned volleyball net that we succeeded in stringing up from the uncovered beams. Yet as the rain continued, we grew irritated by our confinement, and after increasingly desultory play, we would settle down gloomily at the low windows just above the floor, as if they were squashed down by the ends of the steeply slanting beams, and stare out with desperate boredom on the drenched world below, the leaf-crowded, swaying trees, the naked, skeletal piers and diving floats, looking so impermanent from above, and the rain-glazed, empty gray expanse of lake that yielded us nothing.

Then one week end toward the end of the summer Gregory Moore appeared, and he brought Milly a present—a manual on the collection of butterflies and insects, a net, and a cyanide jar. This was a glass cylinder with a screw top, and it brought death without mangling. A half inch of gray powder covered its bottom, and over that was a layer of porous plaster which kept the powder in its place. We were told not to breathe over the jar when it was open, and after Milly's father demonstrated the fascinating effectiveness of the jar with a fly he caught, further admonition was unnecessary. The fly died with a most durable and dizzying leisureliness, a lesson in finality. We spent a happy day with flies alone.

For a few days the sun held, but instead of swimming at last, we caught grasshoppers and June bugs and crickets and various butterflies. There were some large sheets of heavy paper in the Moore attic that we had planned to use for mounting, and it was over these that Freddie and I quarreled and began to fight. I do not remember how this came about, but I suppose, because of its size or condition or some merely imagined advantage, we both wanted the same sheet. Dan was there, but Milly had gone below for a moment, and Freddie had just pulled out the best sheet and given it to Dan, whom, I suppose, he favored. Then we both had hold of the next best sheet, and suddenly we were glaring at each other with resentment, and then anger, and in a minute the paper had been dropped and we were struggling. I can remember now the sensation of my curious, consuming rage, and I can remember feeling the fury of his. It was a battle, and what deep resentments it concealed or what it meant I am unable to say. We were on the floor of that attic, gripped together, rolling back and forth, and slashing out ineffectively until suddenly Freddie hit me maddeningly on the nose. Then, just as my nose began to bleed, I wrested myself free of his arms and, with a lurch, managed to straddle him and pin his arms down with my knees. Purposely I let the blood from my face spatter on his, while he helplessly wrenched his neck back and forth to escape it. His legs were kicking up and down behind me, but I had him firmly on the floor and he could not reach my back. I would have killed him then, if there had been any means, and wildly I thought of the jar, which stood on a table a little away from us, wondering how I could get it and, while he was helpless on his back, press it over his nose and mouth. It was a mad and murderous impulse that I could not attempt to execute since I had to hold him down. He was spitting and shouting with rage, and his face and hair were grotesque with my blood, which had fallen even into his eyes and mouth. Then he gave a great heave, and managed somehow to unseat me, and just as he began to pommel me again, there was another shout—Milly's, a shriek of consternation and her own kind of fury. She seized a broom and with the flat end of it began to beat at both of us. "Help me!" she cried to Dan, who stood by paralyzed with fright, but Freddie and I had already separated, and suddenly our emotions were as limp as our bodies. We looked at each other without feeling anything at all but shame.

Yet what is gained by such an encounter is difficult to estimate: a kind of intimacy of the body, of flesh and breath, that binds as well as severs. I knew him for the first time, with the kind of knowledge one has later of a lover, where hate is intimate and deepest and impossible to abstract. And that was the chief source of our shame.

Milly said curtly, "Go down and wash," and we went down together, and we helped each other, and at the last he looked at me with tears blurring his light brown eyes and said, roughly, "I'm sorry," and I said, "So am I," and the image of his face wavered in my vision. "Here's a comb," he said, and I took it, and handed him a towel.

We went back to the attic slowly and when we got there, Milly merely glanced at us. "We're doing this together, not separately," she said. "The sheets are for different kinds of *things*, not people. We'll have committees. Grant,"—her eyes moved coldly and then kindly over my face—"you're in charge

of collecting. I'll be in charge of killing. Freddie is in charge of
mounting. Dan prints best, so he's in charge of labeling."

"Fair and square," Dan said shakily, and how dark his eyes
were in his still frightened face!

There were two weeks left before Labor Day, and on every
one of these days we were together. The collection grew, and we
even achieved a semblance of order and science on our mounting boards, but as the days dropped away, one after the other,
Freddie sank into a gloom. With every hour summer was dying. I remember Labor Day. We were coming in from a row
on the lake. Dan and I were at the oars, and when we reached
the pier, we got out to make the boat fast. Milly and Freddie
still sat in the back of the boat. He was staring gloomily at
the floor while she explained to him with urgent sweetness that
in winter the rest of us did not see each other either. Over the
shimmering water, a flock of swallows dropped, and shot away,
and we all thought the same thought. Another summer seemed
impossibly distant, you could hardly believe that it could come
at all.

3

It came, of course, the beautiful, hot, high summer of this state, the noblest season, a great green and golden Roman thing at full June opulence when we came again to Silverton. Gregory Moore came too, that summer, with his new wife, Miriam, and a sullen Milly, and his impervious blond sons, who were hardly younger than their new mother. At dusk the great elms around the Moore house attracted a hundred birds, and these at the end of each fair day broke into a desperate competition of song in praise of the day that was ending, a many-throated lyric high and sad and sharply lovely as are all things that help us feel at once life and death together in their true embrace. On our first day back, after supper, the four of us were sitting under the elms, with that torrent of song above us, listening to the notes rising and falling and searching through the air as if to find, if possible, just one new note beyond the liquid patterns to which those small throats were bound, when another voice broke over these. It came floating out through the open French doors of the house, over the terrace, over the lawns, under the trees— the voice of Miriam Moore, singing, I suppose, some *lied*, to an uninsistent piano, and singing like the birds, as if the heart must break with the double stress of joy and sorrow. The voice soared and clung and soared again, rich coloratura, a very presence in the lavender air, an urgent pleading that, in our surprise, pulled us forward toward it where we sat, and then had us up and on our feet. We walked to the terrace and stood at the open doors, looking in at the cavern of the shadowed room. It was lit, in so far as it was lit, by banks of candles that stood in tall holders on either side of the black mass of the piano, each flame long and still and candent in the breathless room. The woman we could not clearly see—only the vagueness of a pale, soft dress, the gleam of shoulders and of pearls perhaps, the dark head; but near the doors sat Gregory Moore, in profile, and we could see his face clearly against the dark of the room as the fading sunlight fell upon it. We had no words for the feeling in that face, for the feeling that pulsated in that room and filled it, but it was more present to us than language could have been. We had come upon the very heart of privacy; we all felt it; simultaneously we dropped back, as if we had been ordered. No one had a right to look upon that face or upon a face like that, scowling without anger, at once naked, ravaged, hungry, gray with adoring. It was the first time that I had seen— these are the little words we later find—the face of a man in thrall.

We dropped back silently and stepped down to the clipped grass, and when we turned to stare at one another in surprise, we saw that there were three of us only, and when we turned to the trees, we saw that Milly was there, had been there all along, looking away from us, leaning against the trunk of a tree, small beside it, as if she were somehow diminished by the trees, or the dusk, or the weight of sound. But now the birds' song was dying, thinning out and settling into fitful chirps, and the woman's voice stopped. We looked back to the black entrances into the room, from which silence now seemed to pour out into the dusk, and then we went back to Milly.

We had no plan, but she said, "Let's go," as if we had, and she said it in the small, despairing voice of one who does not know the luxury of alternative.

We walked home with Dan.

When we remember, we are all at least bad artists, and I may carry with me—the singing birds in the trees, that dark room and the summer twilight, the candles, the music, the singing voice, the stricken, captive face—I may have drawn here (and drawn up from what obscure passages of time and mind?) a very faulty image of love. Yet it is the image that I carry, and it lingers, and in later years I hear her not simply singing, but singing a particular song that, I suppose, I have given her, Wolf's "Und willst du deinen Liebsten sterben sehen," and the thraldom of Gregory Moore, which was in reality a complete gift of his being, has sometimes seemed to me an infinitely desirable state. For I was in time to lose, I do not know how, the ability to be careless of myself.

Bianca and Daniel Ford, Dan's parents, are a different kind of remembrance. That summer, and from then on, with Miriam there, transforming the once casual household into an ordered elegance and creating in her marriage that atmosphere of hot, enchanted privacy, we were not to play much around the Moore house, but seem to have chosen the Fords' instead. And the Fords were like a king and a queen, remarkable in confidence and in the assurance of a superior equality and the sense of their own inevitable rightness; or like, at least, a toy king and a puppet queen, for they were not, I think, without their comic aspect. They were too small as physical beings to assume such enormous complacency as was theirs, so that one had the impression that they could not fill their moral clothing. There were certain affectations—Daniel Ford's dark, solid-colored silk shirts made for him with sleeves a little full and cuffs a little tight, so that they gave the impression of just not being blouses; a beret when he walked; a black beard, pointed and precisely trimmed; and yet with these, denying any mere bohemianism, expensive business suits tailored with

utmost punctilio, or beautifully conservative linen or Palm
Beach or light tweed jackets and knickerbockers. Bianca Ford
might have been his deeply sympathetic sister. She accentuated
the heavy, lily whiteness of her skin by using very dark red lip
rouge and a good deal of dark make-up for her eyes. Her hair
was black, pulled tightly away from her face into an extravagant
chignon that positively hung on her back, and from her ex-
posed ears swung lavish pendant affairs that glowed and flashed.
Her clothes, even her daytime clothes, managed to suggest not
dresses but robes, and her shoes were always colored—green
and purple, garnet, maize, and blue—royal shades. They were
absurdly small people, not more than five feet four or five
inches, and of exactly equal height, and yet, while they were
no doubt regarded as the eccentrics of the summer colony,
theirs was apparently an amiable eccentricity, and no one
laughed at them.

Accepted by others as of at least equal stature, they treated
themselves like royalty. At table, they always sat side by side.
If they were dining alone with Dan, they were together at one
side of the table, Dan opposite them. If they were entertaining,
they were together at one end of the table, the guests dispersed
down the sides. One thought of them as always together, as if,
whenever they appeared, they were making a public appearance
or even a pause in a progress, and one wondered a little what
remnant of regal ceremony they clung to in their most private
interchanges, for I think that they were incapable of abandon-
ing it entirely, lest they should have lost the illusion of divine
right by which they lived.

This I do not of course know, but I believe that they were
a man and woman without passion, a man and woman perfectly matched and perhaps almost entirely unmated. They
created an exotic atmosphere that was yet dry, devoid of
romance, and in this, they were the very opposite of the Moores.

Dan was their only child, yet he seemed not so much their child as their equal, who shared their calm and their equanimity. They preferred each other's company to the company of others, and, without ever exactly shutting themselves off, they lived a little aloof from the rest of the summer colony and always gave their friends a just adequate awareness of their difference. Bianca Ford helped her husband in the management of The Ford Gallery, and thus, unlike other wives and mothers, she not infrequently spent at least part of her week in town with her husband. For brokers and bankers and lawyers and manufacturers, as for their wives, the ownership of an art gallery must in itself have justified a certain eccentricity of dress and conduct and point of view, as Bianca's part in the management of the gallery must have justified her sporadic presence at Silverton and her disinclination to spend her afternoons at the bridge table, or, in 1925, in concentration over a ouija board. The Fords had no questions to ask; they merely averred. *We read, we lounge, we sit together in the sun on a wrought-iron settee, our hands just touching, impassive; we never quarrel, we are in perfect poise, we are right.*

Dan could not judge them, naturally. He was bred without the tools for judgment. Freddie, it developed, loathed his home; Milly yearned for hers, but was denied it; I—well, of that later. But out of one kind of passion or another, out of the kind of grating and disharmony that all passion must entail, each of us fashioned judgment, and a will that would shape action, and in this Dan differed. Yet, being the child, he did not so much aver as accept. His parents had given him nothing to reject, nothing either to yearn for or to deny in them. They gave him the gift of their own kind of confidence; since it was a gift, since he received it only and had not been asked to form it, it was in him necessarily bland, without insistence or force. In friendship he was passive, and therefore to him each of the three of

us was most deeply and intimately drawn. We felt perhaps an
equal friendship, but for Dan we also felt protection.

He was a slight, brown boy, with bright black eyes, and
thick black hair, straight and short like beaver fur. It fit him
like a cap, rounded low over his forehead, curving in at his
temples, and gave him an appearance of exotic distinction. He
had a small brown mole, just darker than his skin, beside his
nose, and his color under the brown was dark red, as if borrowed
from his mother's lips and diffused along the line of his cheekbones. He was a year younger than Freddie and I, with a lighter
and somewhat breathless voice, and even then, when we were
all simple, he was more naïve than we and in a way, therefore,
more sensitive to the condition of others.

We walked along the lake shore through the thickening
gloom. Milly walked shufflingly, with her head down, striking
angrily at bushes and the ground with a stick she carried, and
no one said anything. Freddie tried to whistle, but the bright
notes died tunelessly on his lips. I picked up a white stone and
tossed it in the indigo water. Constraint was heavy, like the
silence between us. Then suddenly Dan skipped a step and said
cheerfully, "My mother plays the harpsichord."

Milly sniffed impatiently.

"In the city, I study the 'cello," he persisted.

"Who doesn't know that?" and *whissh!* she brought her
stick down through the air.

Dan hesitated, and then blurted bravely, "I'm studying a
Haydn bourrée."

No one took him up. Now we had come to the Fords', and
we stood on the grass beside an iron deer that glittered darkly
in the lights that fell aslant from the house through the trees.
Milly wove her arms in the cold, rounded horns, and wound
her fingers among the well-rubbed tines, so that she looked as
though she hung there helplessly and would be tossed and

gored by the iron thing. On the darkened lake a launch coughed and sputtered and gave a distant roar, then raced off into a diminishing hum. Far off somewhere a man's voice rang out over the water, and from a pier nearby laughter lightly died. Along the shore, yellow light lay uneasily on the water in reflected swathes, and the evening bats swept and circled over them in their restless hunt for insects. In the distance a phonograph played a spasmodic song, and from the broad porch of the Ford house a Negro voice called softly, "Master Dan, it's time."

Milly's arms slipped down and she put her head on the cold arched neck of the deer and began to cry. Her thin shoulders shook on the inflexible shoulders of the deer, and the muffled sound of her sobs said that she must have been biting into the flesh of her arm to subdue them. No one had ever seen her like this, and none of us knew what to do. We inched toward her stiffly, and hesitated. "God damn it, God damn it!" she began to say through her broken sobs. Then she straightened up and impatiently wiped her arm across her eyes.

Freddie spoke first. "Gosh," he said, "when I was a kid, I used to run away from home, just go poking around town, and you know what my mother did? She got some rope and she tied me up to a post in the back yard, with about ten feet around the post to play in, like a dog on a leash, one whole summer. . . . Talk about tough!"

It was the first time that Freddie had told us about his home. Dan stared at him and Milly looked at him obliquely, doubtfully. His revelation made me bold. "My mother drinks," I said.

Milly sniffed again. "Everybody drinks."

"Too much, I mean," I said.

"Master Dan! Master Dan!" The soft dark voice came through the darkness like a kiss.

"Coming."

We walked up the lawn to the porch with him. "Tomorrow . . ." Milly started.

Then two voices said "Hello" together, and we looked up. On one of the wrought-iron balconies which hung suspended from the upper windows of the house stood the Fords. They were framed in an opening filled with golden light and bounded by the scallop shape of heavy drapery. We could not see their faces, only their black silhouettes cut sharply out of the yellow light as they stood there together, two benign presences, like some coupled statue not quite life size from antiquity. "Hello," they said again, together, as if they had rehearsed.

"Hello," we said.

"It's late, Dan," his father said in his soft burring voice, and "Nearly nine," his mother said in the tone of one who confers a blessing.

"I'm coming up now," he said in happy acquiescence, and turning to us, "See you tomorrow." Then he went quickly across the wide porch, and into the house.

For a moment we stood and watched the door into which he had disappeared. Then we looked up and saw that his parents had gone back in, and through the lighted doors that opened on the balcony, we heard muted laughter and Dan's voice. Then the draperies fell across the opening and it was dark as the night around.

"I have to go back," Milly said. "See you tomorrow." She turned swiftly, as if with a resolution, and vanished spectrally among the trees.

"My bike's in front," Freddie said.

"I'm going this way," I said.

We said good night, and I went back to the path along the shore. Water lapped mournfully against the piers, and the phonograph music sounded nearer. I cut up through a meadow that lay between the Fords' house and my father's, and, through a place I had worn and regularly used, crept under the hedge that separated the meadow from our lawn. On my knees, I saw that the first floor of our house was lighted up. The music came from the living room, and people moved across the windows, dancing. I was about twenty feet from a porch attached to the side of the house, and as I knelt in the damp grass, debating which way to enter, a shadow separated itself from the shadowy trellis of roses that covered the southern end of the porch. It was a man's figure, moving stealthily, and then seating itself on the railing. The man struck a match to light a cigarette, and I saw that it was my father. I stiffened, and knelt still. Then a burst of laughter came from the open windows, and a new record sounded out. It was "Whispering," and through the windows I saw my mother dancing with one of the Moore boys. She wore a pink dress and, for some reason, a large pink hat with a droopy brim, and it seemed to me that she had difficulty in keeping the hat on her head while she danced. Laughter bubbled up over the beat of the song. My father's cigarette glowed. Then it came toward me through the darkness in an arch, as he flipped it away. It hissed softly in the damp grass and went out. The music stopped and someone started it again, and again my mother and the Moore boy seemed to be the only ones who were dancing. They pranced to the thin music of "Whispering," and the brim of the pink hat flopped on my mother's yellow hair, and presently it fell off as she whirled. It was a transparent hat, like the hats that bridesmaids often wear, and it sailed off to spastic words that reached across the garden . . . *that you'll never grieve me* . . . *whisper . . . never leave me . . . whispering.* . . .

I knelt in the grass for a long time and watched my father watching my mother. Every now and then he lit a new cigarette, and I would see the ruddy flash of his face, or part of it, and

the glowing butts always came shooting over to me, as if he
were signaling to me in a conspiracy. Did I feel anything—
for him? for her? I remember only that my knees grew stiff
and aching and that I was shivering in the soft, summer night.
Inside, the music stopped, and the pink figure of my mother
disappeared, and the shadow of my father remained motion-
less on the porch. A glass shattered with a sharp sound. Voices
rose. My mother laughed, and, not seeing her, I thought the
laughter sounded deep and wild. At last I got stiffly to my feet
and moved cautiously along against the darkness of the hedge
until I could dart safely across the gravel drive to the back door
of the house and get up to my room by the servants' stairs.

How, without revelations that are rare, can we know our
parents? Or is that quite what I mean? I should have asked:
how can we look back and say, ah! this was the pressure of the
casual thumb on the clay that, once the casting was complete,
left *that* inflexible feature in the bronze of my will. And what
we forget! All that we cannot bear to know that we cannot live
with. Yet live with it we do, and the will is bronze because we
do not know, we cannot remember, why it wills as it does. We
forget how we feel, and, for the feeling that even then was making us, we retain only, we substitute the mute and bearable tokens, a pink hat or a wisp of song or an iron deer in the darkness,
spice odors of melancholy leaking from closed cupboards.

This I know. I had had a younger sister, Lucy, who was
born five years after me, and who died accidentally as an infant.
I hardly remember this child, but I seem to have a memory of
my mother as different in my early youth, before that death.
I think of a tall blond girl—yes, a girl!—with an easy, swinging
walk, a careless girl who brought into our life from the California ranch on which she was born and lived as a child an air of
freedom and spaciousness, and with that, an easygoing stri-

dency, too, a certain generous brashness. She always moved, even later, as though she were walking along a road or crossing an open field, and she talked, not loudly, but yet as though she were out-of-doors. From Mexican ranch hands she had learned to play the guitar, and to this she sang their songs of luxuriating sorrow in her coarse, untrained, and strangely moving alto. She rode with natural ease and dash, but with humorous contempt for the English style and Eastern horses. After the death of her child, she ceased to ride, and she seldom touched the guitar on which summer dust collected in the garden house, where it hung over the fireplace; her careless ease turned to laxity, and more and more she gave herself to abrupt and jarring harshness of judgment.

She had taken the child, less than a year old, to the edge of the lake, where she was in the habit of undressing it and sunning it, while she lay in the sun herself; but on this day, as she lay on her back, remembering, possibly, curving, golden ranges or Sierra skies, she dozed, and slept, and when she woke, the child's blanket was an empty, rumpled square, and the child was dead in the lapping water's shallow edge, where it had rolled or crept, and a celluloid rattle floated beside it.

Another man might have saved her from the course she took, but my father must have been alarmed by her grief or intimidated by the dumbness of her self-reproach to a degree that left him helpless to counter either with love, and deference was then of no use to her. So the death of this child—and I do not know what else—pushed them apart, pushed her into those sickening frivolities of which a restless drunkenness was only one, pushed him, finally, into suspicious brooding, watching, and self-immolating slackness. There was no quarrel between them, no open conflict, but a gap, and this she filled with the easy and inadequate materials of those queer years. She was then thirty-seven or thirty-eight. At night, when she was in the house, the phonograph hardly ever stopped playing. It played on and on that night—"Whispering" again and again, and "Genevieve," and "When My Baby Smiles at Me"—on and on as I lay on my back in bed and coldly reflected on my father lurking indecisively on the porch by the rose trellis.

I slept, and much later I awoke with a start. At first I did not know what had troubled my sleep, but then I heard the voices on the drive below, singing over the sound of a racing motor, the voices of young men. The singing died out on the highway and the sound of the motor diminished to a hum, and nothing. Then the heavy predawn summer silence closed down on the house. I heard electric switches clicking off below, and then my mother's slow climbing step on the stairs. I could picture her, pulling herself wearily up along the banister, tottering in pink satin slippers. She was sobbing softly. Then these sounds stopped, and I knew that she was standing outside my door. I lay absolutely still. The door creaked open slowly, held, and then closed again. She went with lagging steps across the wide corridor to her room, and I heard her door close after her. No one followed.

Some separation took place between them and me. I had been through the stage of imagining ways and devices whereby I might help them. I had been through a short-lived stage of desperately praying that God help them. I had been lonely because of them. But now as I lay in the darkness, I accepted loneliness, I accepted separation. I thought, I don't need them, either of them; I have friends. I was not unhappy. I fell asleep again, indeed, in the very happy illusion that love can be a choice before it is a capacity.

There were other children in that summer colony, of course, but except for some of their names, I remember little about them beyond the self-satisfying derision in which we held them, and especially Milly's passionate dislike for girls, an attitude that, at our age, made her only the more acceptable to us. She strove to excel, when she needed to strive, in every boys' activity and in the special knowledges of boys. That summer we all had air rifles—Milly, too—and soon her aim was as good as Freddie's, and the two of them liked to try to pick off sparrows from telephone wires, and occasionally managed. I was much less accurate, and Dan could not bring himself to shoot at live things; he practiced with tin cans on fence posts, and could make them go *ping, ping, ping* in a rapid succession of shots.

That summer, too, we built a raft according to specifications that Milly had found in *Popular Mechanics*—an ambitious craft designed to convey us up and down the small river that has its source at the head of the lake. Our first project was an overnight camping trip to a place called Picnic Bluff, and it was only after the raft was finished and our supplies were nearly assembled that Mrs. Colby took Milly's casually announced plan seriously enough to report it to her father and her stepmother, who, of course, told her that naturally it was an impossible idea, one girl out all night with three boys. Milly said, "Don't worry," to us, and, "All right, just for the day, then," to them, and we completed our preparations.

The lake houses were still closed in sleep and silence on the morning that we started. It was hardly five o'clock, the sun was just up, a pink flush fading in the sky over the eastern hills, and silvery mists were lifting along the shores of the lake like veils from ladies' green faces. Now and then a bird went skimming over the water, but nothing else stirred. We poled our way silently along the shore and into the wide shallow opening of the river, under the great overhanging willows that grew there, and then, as if we had made a successful escape, we began to shout and sing. Dan, who had been reading Mark Twain, had got himself up to look something like Huck Finn, with patched overalls and a checked shirt, a frayed straw hat and a corncob pipe. The rest of us, tolerant of his attraction to such literary mummery, accepted the pipes he had brought along for us. He had a can of something that we called Indian tobacco, the product of a common weed whose blossom dried into a mahogany-colored nubbly stuff that you could strip off the stalk with your hands and that burned easily. We smoked our pipes, and we worked our poles in the shallow water, and when the sun was well up, we undressed down to swimming suits and occasionally we swam along beside the raft or pushed it, or we would tie it up to a tree and dive off it for a while. At noon we ate clumsy sandwiches of sausage and cheese that I had made the night before, and we drank lemonade from a thermos bottle supplied by the Fords.

The place we had in mind was a broad shelf of sand bar sloping up to a narrow strip of scrubby trees directly under steeply overhanging limestone cliffs. On top of the cliffs was a village picnic grounds with a bandstand, but the place that we had chosen below was nearly inaccessible except from the river itself. It was only three or four miles up the river, but it took us most of the day to get there. When we arrived, we beached our raft and made our camp. Dan had brought his BB gun, and he tacked a target up on a tree and practiced his aim while the rest of us fished, and Milly and Freddie each caught a perch which they cleaned for our supper. We built a fire at the edge of the trees, and ate, and then lay on our blankets watching the daylight fade out over the water and our fire redden in the dusk.

Dan bored us with a detailed plot summary of *The Barber of Seville*. His parents frequently took him to hear opera, and there were long family sessions beforehand over the libretto and a careful study of themes at the piano, so that he was an expert of a kind that we were not, and often made us impatient with his special cultivation. Still, with that deference we had for him, we listened, and, free there and together by the fire in the summer twilight, we all felt happy and relaxed and life could not have seemed better as his light, breathless voice raced on. ". . . Then there is this girl, her name is Rosina. . . ."

But presently Milly broke in. "Let's talk about Dumas. Let's talk about *The Man in the Iron Mask*."

"Or let's fence," Dan cried, and leapt up and seized a stripped willow branch from the sand. "*Touché!*"

"Oh, sit down, Dan," Milly told him, and we talked about Dumas, and dungeons, and torture, and somehow we came to the subject of blood brotherhood.

It was late now, ten o'clock or half-past ten, and we were rolled up in our blankets under the trees, our feet pointing to the fire. It had settled down to a red glare without flames, yet it cast a pink glow up through the thin tree trunks, onto the pale face of the cliff behind us, and marked our place in the thick, surrounding darkness. Milly was saying, "Some tribes have a ceremony where they drink the blood, but others. . . ."

Dan broke in sleepily. "What's that sound?"

It was what seemed to be the miles-distant mutter of an outboard motor. "A boat out on the lake," I told him. But suddenly, with a shift of breeze, the sound seemed much nearer, and then came an unmistakable call in the night. "Hal-loo-oo," it went and again, "Hal-loo-oo," a long, melancholy wail in the night.

Milly struggled up and sat staring hard out at the river. "That's not on the lake," she said.

The putt-putt of the motor was distinctly nearer, and again the voice called out, like a cry from a lost soul, "Hal-loo-oo, hal-loo-oo. . . ."

We were all sitting up now. "Scary," Dan said. "What is it, do you think?"

Freddie knew first. "It's people looking for us, I'll bet."

"For me," Milly said quietly. "Oh, of course, damn them, not for you, but for *me!*"

The sound of the motor labored nearer in the darkness, and the voice called out again and again, more human now and more purposeful, and then we saw a yellow glimmer of lights through the screen of willows at the point where the sand bar began.

"Put out the fire!" Milly whispered. "Quick!"

"Too late," said Freddie, and the boat came gliding like a slow shadow around the bend below us, a lantern at its bow and its stern. A woman's voice called sharply, "There, Greg, there!"

"Oh, damn, damn, damn," Milly moaned, and threw herself back on the sand. The motor cut off with a splutter, the boat slid toward the shore, and, when it scraped on the sand, two figures jumped out.

"Milly, are you there?" her father called.

Dan and Freddie and I shook ourselves out of our blankets and stood up, but Milly turned over on the sand, face down. "She's here," we said.

They came running awkwardly up through the loose sand and peered at us in the dim light of the fire. "Where?" Miriam Moore cried, but Milly's father had seen her stretched taut on the sand, and he was kneeling beside her, with his hands on her. "Come on, Milly," he said, angrily. "You had no—"

But he got no further. Milly struggled away from him, freed herself from her blanket, and leapt up. She ran to a tree behind her and threw her arms around its trunk and cried, "I won't go! I won't! You can't make me!"

He shouted her name in angry surprise, and with depressing deliberation began to walk toward her, where she clung to the tree.

"No, wait," his wife said. "Greg, wait." She ran after him

and went to Milly. "Milly, dear, come along now," she said pleasantly, "like a good child."

Milly turned her face toward the cliff. "Go away," she said passionately. "I'm *not* coming."

"Baby—please." Miriam Moore said it very gently and put her arm across Milly's shoulder. Then Milly flew to pieces, all splitting, electric nerves. She let go of the tree and struck the arm from her shoulder and leapt back and her body, wiry and thin as a boy's, seemed, in the dim light, to shake with rage and indignation, like her voice, as she screamed, "Don't you touch me! Don't *you* dare touch me!"

The hate in her voice pushed Miriam Moore back a step or two, as a blow might have, and Gregory Moore rushed forward. She stopped him again, and spoke softly to him. "I can't, I guess, after all. But be gentle with her, for heaven's sake. Nothing else. Just gentle. Please."

And when her father went to her then and, in the tenderest possible voice, said, "Come home now, Milly," the tautness left her body and she looked up at him miserably and began simply to cry. He picked her up as if she were an infant, and as they passed between us to go back to the boat, with Miriam Moore a step or two behind, Milly's sobs subsided and sounded no more like weeping but like the dejected whimpering of an injured animal. Her father put her into the boat and came back for her blanket. He looked at us, still standing there, and said in a pleasantly gruff way, "You boys want to push us off?" and went back again. Miriam Moore sat by the motor, and Milly and her father together in the middle seat. Milly seemed shrouded in the blanket, in the protection of his arm, and if she looked at us, we could not see her. We shoved the boat off the sand. Its lanterns cast rippled reflections in the water and picked out, in ghostly gray, the delicate drooping branches of the willows on the shore. The motor coughed and caught, and the boat turned slowly round, and moved away. We stood and listened as the sound faded, and our eyes got used to the darkness.

We came back late in the afternoon of the next day, and Milly was waiting for us on the Ford pier. She must have seen us poling along the shore for at least a half mile, but she made no effort to meet us, and as we came up to the pier, she still did not move, but sat staring glumly at us from one of the two benches at the end.

"Hi—Milly?" Dan called.

She stared and stood up and slouched to the post near the shore where we were tying up the raft. "What did you do today?" she asked.

Dan began, "This morning, we—"

But she cut him off. "We're going to Europe."

We stared back at her. At last Freddie said, "You mean, in September?"

"No, next week. It's all settled. My father telephoned the steamship company this morning. We won't be back here this summer."

"Why?" we asked. "Why so sudden?"

Milly was standing on the pier above us, looking down. Now she looked away. "They think they can break this up."

"What?"

"This. Us."

"Oh."

"I have to go to the village now—with—her. To get some stuff." Then her thin, miserable face brightened a little. "But will you meet me here after dinner? Freddie—can you?"

"Sure."

"Good. Then be here."

And when we met again she led us mysteriously to a thicket

of apple trees in a deserted orchard, and there she produced a razor blade with which she made each of us cut the palm of his right hand. Then each of us shook hands with the others and at the end all the right hands were clasped together in a knot. It was very solemn and rather messy. "Now you have to protect that hand," Milly enjoined us at last. "Do not wash it. You have to let the blood wear off by itself."

4

She vanished from that summer. They tried with good hearts but too late to draw her into their hot intimacy, the enveloping aura of engrossed attraction that was their marriage, yet that bond of passionate attentiveness was by its very nature exclusive. Wonderful for them, for Milly it could have been taken only in some other way: the closer she came to it, the more sharply it expelled her, and the summer shaped her independence.

Uncommunicative postcards came to each of us now and then from Baden-Baden and Cernobbio, and they always said the same thing, "Say hello to—" and then named the other two, and no more. The summer burned away. That September I was sent to school in New Hampshire. Freddie sank back into the dead winter of Silverton. Milly was in Albany. Dan lived in the Eighties, and even when I had been in the city during the winter, we had never seen each other. The whole reason could not have been that our house was on Waverly Place, so far downtown. That friendship was a summer and a country thing. In the next summer it went on as if there had been no interruption, although for the first month Dan was not there, but with his mother and father in Paris. They came to Silverton just before the Fourth of July.

I remember this because my mother gave a party for young and old, an enormous informal affair held on the shore between the garden house and the water. Japanese lanterns were strung from the trees, a fire blazed in the yellow evening light, long tables covered with white linen were set out on the grass, loaded with food and liquor, china and glassware and silver, and in the garden house a small orchestra played the tunes that punctuated that summer, and people danced. In the intervals, musicians dressed as gypsies wandered through the crowd with stringed instruments, and one of them sang melancholy waltzes in a trembling tenor. Still later, when the fire had died down and the darkness was complete, there were fireworks. These had been put in my charge, and Freddie and Milly helped me, and Dan was there, standing by. We tacked pinwheels to a tree trunk near the water and set them spinning. Fountains of colored flame danced up from Roman candles stuck in the wet sand. Rockets sprayed out over the lake like hissing stars, and some made triangles and squares, flowers bursting into a brief, geometric life, and at last, a flag—red, white, and blue —that stood in the air for a little while, a gaudy vision, before it wavered and melted and flowed away into darkness.

After that, the music took up loudly again, the younger children were taken away, a crowd quickly gathered at the table with the liquor, and we four sat by ourselves among our burnt debris on the pebbly beach. Behind us, on the sloping grass, a bank of adults sat in scattered groups, and between the irregular alternations of music, jazz tunes and false gypsy songs, we heard their low laughter and talk and ice rattling in their glasses, and occasionally, my mother's strident laugh above the other sounds. Presently there was more urgent talk behind us and her laughing response, and then she took the guitar from the warbling tenor and played it. In a white voile dress, with her head thrown back, she walked slowly back and forth along the shore, singing hoarsely:

> *La noche 'sta serena,*
> *Tranquilo el aquilon,*

Tu dulce centinela,
Te guarda el corazon. . . .

She returned the guitar, and she listened to the applause and the murmuring approval, and then cried, "Oh God, how boring! And it's hot!" and kicked off her shoes and strode purposefully to the pier and out to its end and dived off into the black water. There was a gasp and uneasy laughter. I didn't know where my father was—was he there at all?—but a few other men ran out to the end of the pier where they could see her bare white arms breaking the black water, and then they were kneeling on the planks and, in the light of the paper lanterns that were strung down the length of the pier, were helping her up the ladder. Freddie was standing, staring, his mouth open, beside me. Milly and Dan were silent. A woman's voice behind me said, "What's boring is Ellen, with her grandstanding." I had never before felt such total indifference, both to this and to my mother herself, as she came back then, leaning on the men around her, laughing, her hair streaming, her white dress plastered to her body. It was not I but Dan who said, in a tight, embarrassed voice, "Let's go up to the orchard."

Our orchard was an old, neglected patch of apple trees that grew in a meadow between the back part of the house and the highway. In an earlier summer, we had contrived a primitive system of parallel bars in the gnarled branches of three or four trees, and it was a place we liked, because it was at once near our houses and yet always deserted, the scene of our pact. Only we went there. We sprawled out now in the long grass at the edge farthest from the house. Away from the lights and the party, we could see the bright stars scattered over the immense sky.

"Polaris. The Pole Star," Dan said, pointing up. "The star you sail by."

We lay on our backs, hands under our heads. Dan moved, and pointing to the southwest, he said, "Venus. Venus is blue. No one has ever seen Venus because of the clouds around it, but it's most like the earth."

"How do they know, if they haven't seen it?"

"They know."

"How?"

"I don't know. But they do. It's so much like earth that there may be people like ourselves there."

"Ahh—"

"Yes," he said.

"Why should there be?"

"Well, the clouds mean that there's water, and where there's water, there could be people like us."

"Ahh—"

"Yes," he said again. He stood up and pulled himself up on one of the bars in the tree nearest us. He sat on it, and then swung round and hung by his knees and craned his neck to look at the sky upside down.

"If you look this way, you see shapes."

"What shapes?" one of us asked without interest. We three, lying close together in the grass, each aware of the others' breathing bodies, were feeling our older emotions. Dan *was* the youngest.

"Shapes," he said, "like those the rockets made. Hang up here—you see these things!"

Milly, beside me, said, "Squint your eyes down here, it looks the same way."

"Squares and triangles. . . ."

"Yes!" she said. "If you squint, the stars all put themselves into shapes, squares and triangles and wheels. . . ."

The bar that Dan was hanging on creaked in the branches as he dropped to the ground. He flung himself down and after a moment cried, "Yes, that's it! See? You see it all in shapes!"

Then we all lay on our backs and squinted at the sky, and it was true, the stars fell into patterns, and they did look, indeed, like the simple forms left in the sky by the spurting rockets when their first lavish flare thinned out, but fixed forever in their rigid designs, bright, complacent specks strung on invisible lines of vastly distant fixity!

"You can almost see the lines," I said.

"Lines?"

"The lines that make the shapes—squares, triangles. . . ."

"Are lives," Milly asked, as if she had misunderstood my word, "are lives tied on wheels?"

No one answered, no one understood for the moment, perhaps. We lay still and stared up at the black dome fitted with its brilliant, necessitarian array.

"Lines," I said at last. "I said '*lines*.' Like in science books, where they draw in the lines of the constellations so you can see the shape."

"But I meant lives." Her voice was small. "Are lives tied to wheels?" She sounded distant, not next to me, queer, and her question or the voice in which she asked it made me feel alone and queer. I moved my arm and let my hand lie on Freddie's shoulder.

"What wheels?" he asked.

"I mean—" We waited for her to go on, and in the silence we heard the distant, ghostly rhythms, hardly more than the beat-beat-beat of a song called "I Won't Say I Will, but I Won't Say I Won't." They were still dancing at my mother's party, and I wondered idly whether she had changed her dress, and if she had, what dress she was wearing now, and the soft heat of the summer night seemed slowly to gather together and press down on me where I lay. Then I felt my own fingers

moving restlessly and independently of any volition on the
curve of Freddie's shoulder, and I took my hand away.

"I mean—" Her voice rose a little with the effort of her
thought. "Like the stars. See—they're all tied to those shapes.
They have to stay that way. They all move only as the shape
moves. Or really, they don't move at all, it's the earth that
moves. But the earth, too, it can't move except in the track, on
its wheel, like. Are lives like that? That's what I mean."

Dan sat up. "If a tree falls in the forest," he said eagerly,
"and there's no one there to hear it, does it make a sound? Does
it?"

"That's different," she said patiently. "I mean: do we live
the way we do because we have to, or because we want to?"

"What's fate?" Dan asked. "What is it, anyway?"

Freddie spoke. "Fate is what happens to you. The opposite
is will. Will is what you make happen."

"That's it," she said. "Do we really make things happen,
make our lives, our selves, or are they made for us?"

"We make them," Freddie said, and he sat up.

"But how do you ever know?" she persisted.

"Well, like—" He started and stopped. "Well, I do," he
insisted. "Like—what I wanted most of all a couple of years
ago was to know you. If I'd gone on just wishing, it would
never have happened. You have to *do* something about it. So
I hung around where I knew you sometimes went. And you
came. See? Also, I knew you were city kids and wouldn't just
take up with me if I didn't have something to make *you* want
to. See? It works both ways. So I brought that slingshot. Remember? And it was easy as anything." He laughed with deep
warmth in his recollection.

Milly sat up. Reflectively, she said, "I never did learn to hit
a bird!" and Freddie laughed again. She looked at him closely,

leaning toward him in the darkness. "And can you always do that? Make what you want to happen, happen?"

"Sure."

"But you have parents. They have something to say."

"They don't care. They care less and less. See, you get older, you get freer—"

"I don't. Mine interfere more and more, instead of less and less."

"But you care less, because what they want doesn't have anything to do at all with what *you* want, and because it doesn't really change anything that you want, and when you get free, you'll *be* what you want."

"When do you get free?" she asked, and once more her voice had gone small and queer, tight with some pain.

Only I lay on my back now. The others sat up around me, alert with their talk. I lay there feeling numb and apart from them, unattached, and as I stared up at the limitless vault of black sky and the glimmering stars, my throat constricted, and I wanted to cry out to them: *But is that what we want, to be free? do we want to be free?* I turned over so that I would not suddenly sob, and then slowly, as I lay there, with the distant, rapid thrum-thrum-thrum-thrum-thrum of "Stumbling" beating on the night air, all that loose, enervating melancholy that ached in and, as it were, around me in the immediate darkness, drew itself together and tightened in me, almost as if it were a matter of nerves and muscles, and I felt my body grow quiet and come to some hard rest.

Something had happened to Milly, too. She leapt to her feet and did a few quick turns on the bar and then dropped briskly to the ground and said, "I have to go. She said to be in by eleven." She said it almost without resentment, with none of her usual cutting emphasis on the "she," with the kind of acceptance in her voice that must have meant that she had, in a measure, won a freedom through Freddie's assurances, that she, like others, saw and held a future.

"I'll go with you," he said. Was it a new, proprietory tone he used? Had we all changed there, in that brief and childish colloquy on the stars? Apparently not, or not Dan, at any rate, who said now with his usual blandness, "Well, we'll all go, won't we?" And we all went, very much as usual, through the dark orchard, across the lighter meadow, past the Fords', on to the shore, and toward the great, dim windows of the Moores' house, where Milly disappeared through draperies, gray in the night, that billowed out momentarily like mist, then hung still.

We walked back to the Fords'. Freddie got on his bicycle and wheeled whistling down the drive to the highway, and Dan and I stared up at the house, which was silent and only dimly lit with night lights.

"They're not home yet," he said. The sounds of laughter and music at our house persisted. "Let's go down to the pier."

We sat on a bench at the end of the Ford pier. Here the stars seemed to have faded, and the lake was black everywhere except over at our pier, where the lanterns made colored splashes on the lighter surface. Staring at those lights, I thought that again I could feel the night grow closer, hotter, and I said, "I'm going swimming."

"Yes. Let's," Dan said. We took off our clothes and dived into the water, and we swam quietly out from the end of the pier, then back, floated idly on our backs for a while, spouted water, and climbed out. Then we sat naked on the end of the pier, our feet dangling over the edge, touching the water, and we shivered with a kind of luxury as the soft air dried us. My hands lay in my loins. The music sounded across the water—the throbbing piano and drums, the mooning tenor saxophone, and the cutting, climbing, obbligato horn. Something happened again: the notes of the music reached me, reached into me, and prodded that melancholy ache of the orchard into a vicious clutching that was like hatred, if hatred can be of the flesh. At the same time, under my hands, there was a stirring that was now part of the hatred. I waited while this perverse excitement grew like a violent stranger outside me who would suddenly speak, and then, when Dan began to speak, saying dreamily, "Sometimes—" I swung toward him abruptly and said, "Do you do this?" and with quick thrusts showed him what I meant. In the darkness, his face was only a blur, and I could not see his eyes at all, but I could visualize their wounded widening and surprise from his voice, which said distantly, weakly, "You and Freddie—" and stopped, and started again, "I haven't hardly got any hair there yet," and turned his head.

His mildness was suddenly outrageous to me: it gave me, at last, a target, I suppose, and all of whatever it was that troubled me, crowded into a vicious, panted whisper, in a double release, "You stinking little Christer!"

He sat quietly beside me for a minute or two, his face turned away. The music had stopped, and in the silence I could feel him trying to understand this violation of his innocence in my sudden tortured attack. At the same time, wondering why I had done it, I felt feeling diffuse itself in me again, drain rapidly away, until once more, as previously in the orchard, I was numb and utterly unattached, but in addition, ashamed. Then, quietly, Dan swung up to his feet and picked up his clothes.

"Where are you going?" I managed.

He kept on walking. His steps made the pier vibrate gently. Then he was off it, gone. And then I let my rage, mixed now with remorse, burst out. Or rather, it was as if rage and remorse took hold of me and controlled me, shook me and wracked me, threw me down on the wet boards and rained blows on me, howled for me in the salty, empty darkness, until I escaped from under the torrent at last and slid into the water and swam again, alone now, and sick of feeling.

Next morning I went straight to Dan's house and told him that I was sorry. He looked at me with perfect friendliness and said, "Forget it." Thus, no harm had been done. Perhaps good came of it: that was the last time I cried. Tears, I mean.

5

But this eye should be more neutral. I let myself speak too much *of* myself, who am of least importance. Already I was breaking away from them, writing, in those moments of isolated pain and struggle, my declaration of independence, such as it was to be—wanting more than they had. Summer was no longer, for me, a separate season, and I began to bring into it, in a way that the other three somehow did not, the demands and the lessons of the winter. In the next summer, this difference became clear. In that New Hampshire town where I went to school, there was, for example, a girl who for fifty cents would meet any older boy behind a boarded-up refreshment stand at the outer edge of a park that was itself on the edge of the village. I was sixteen that winter, and when I came to Silverton in the next summer, I was different.

Winter had changed me, and I knew it when I looked at Milly. Something physical happened to me then, in that sixteenth summer, an ache in my throat, an almost sickening emptiness in my stomach, and some kind of glaze over my eyes. Until that summer I had felt about her exactly as I felt about the two boys who now lay stretched on their backs in the long grass behind the log on which she sat. Dan and Freddie and Milly and Grant: until this summer there had been no distinction: all equal, all friends. Now there was a difference. I wondered whether Dan and Freddie felt it too, whether, when they looked at Milly now, they felt as I did, as though someone had punched them hard in the belly. Milly, I thought from a certain strain between us, knew that something had changed.

She had changed, of course. Under her boy's blue shirt, breasts that a tight brassière could not suppress rose and fell. The sleeves of her shirt were rolled up high, and there was something moving in her thin, brown arms alone. She was sitting on a log with her knees apart and her elbows planted on her knees and her chin thrust into her hands, and, still wearing dungarees, as we were, she looked in some ways like an angry boy, but her lips were parted like a woman's, and her eyes were not a child's. Her face was dark with brooding of a quality that was not suited to its puerile source, or to her language. "This morning she said I was a disgrace to what she calls my '*sex*'! Maybe I am. But why doesn't she lay off? It's *her* 'sex,' anyway, not mine."

"Aw, mothers!" Freddie said.

"*Step*mothers!" she corrected him with vicious emphasis, and her chin grew pointed in her anger.

"Well, fathers, for that matter!" I said.

She lifted her head and turned to me with a question on her lips, and the full sight of her face, her anger suddenly gone and interested sympathy there instead, made me suck in my breath. I forgot what I had meant to say.

"Fathers . . ." she said softly, half question, half reflection. For the first time, I knew that what I really wished was that the other boys were not there, that they would go away. I wanted her alone.

We were all together, spread out there on the bottom of a pit. It was an old quarry, abandoned years before we were born, and a place that we had always enjoyed. Dan had a real rifle now, a .22 single shot, and he lay on his stomach, arms and gun propped up on a log, shooting across the quarry at one of the small paper targets with which he seemed always to be supplied. Of the four of us, he was the best shot, and he took some pleasure in the precision of his aim for itself alone that the rest of us, who borrowed the gun to take a shot at a rabbit or a squirrel, did not feel. It was like the pleasure that a musician must enjoy, a violinist when his bow strikes the strings with absolute perfection, or a pianist when his hands come down in sharp and exact chordal unity, or the pleasure that anyone feels who finds his joy entirely in an act alone, and needs no consequences to round it out. We three, in our desultory talk, watched him idly in his concentration. The morning sunshine here was like a lazy prisoner and lay inert on ground and stagnant pools of rain water, rocks, weeds, daisies, scrub oak, and a clump of birch. On three sides, walls of naked, weathered yellow limestone stood up steeply for perhaps a hundred feet, and on the fourth side, a wooded, gravelly slope threaded with paths slanted down to us from the rolling fields above. On two of the walls, we had often climbed from top to bottom and from bottom to top. They were rough with broken rock that offered ample holds for hands and feet, and the sides had a mild slope that let us press against the rock. But the fourth side, the northern side, had almost no slope at all and it was less scarred. We had often lounged below it as we did now, and we had talked of climbing it, we had mapped imaginary climbs up its face and finally the one possible climb, but we had never gone more than a few feet up and never down it at all, and none of us had ever challenged any of the others to try. This day was to mark that difference, too.

"I don't want my hair touched. I don't need a manicure. The dress she bought is awful. I don't want to go to that dance." All this in a burst, bitterly spoken.

"But you are going, Milly?" I asked, studying her, and seeing again how little indeed she looked like all those other young girls who were mad to be allowed to go to dances and strove to appear as much as possible like their young mothers.

"No," she said without conviction.

"Give in," Freddie said, rolling over on his side and looking up at her. "Give in on stuff like that. It doesn't matter. Why fight with them over what doesn't matter? I'd like to go if I could."

"You can!" she said indignantly.

"No. . . ."

"Of course! *I've* asked you. It's our dance. It's *for* me, really—though they don't say so. To make me ladylike!"

"Your mother doesn't want me to come. She hasn't asked me."

"She hasn't asked Dan or Grant either. None of the young —only the grownups."

"Well, are you going?" Freddie asked.

It was a way out. She said, "I won't go if you don't come."

"I'll come," he said, and I saw the sudden brightness break across his broad features and light up his eyes, which had been sullen all that morning. For him, it did matter, and my momentary irritation with him on that account made me say the reckless thing that I then said and was presently to regret.

"Freddie, I dare you to climb the north end. But I bet you won't!" There was malice in the challenge, I know, an emotion that was related in some way to that more childish rage that made me fight with him in the first summer we knew him.

He looked at me in surprise and I tried to look back coolly. "Or will you?"

"Gee, why should he?" Dan asked, and then, with his love of amity, quickly said, "Gee, remember *Tom Swift in the Rockies?* Remember when—"

"Will *you?*" Milly asked me, and her blue eyes took my measure with a kind of hostility.

"Yeah, *will* you?" Freddie asked at once.

"I put the dare," I said as blithely as I could.

Milly leapt to her feet and said, "I will," and she turned to study the steep north end of the quarry for a moment. Then she began to walk toward it.

I went after her and seized her arm. "Milly, don't do it. That was a stupid thing for me to say."

She turned and looked at me with the faintest contempt. We were standing very close to each other, looking straight into each other's eyes, and then there was a pull between us, a sudden dancing, magnetic thing. I said, "Please, Milly, don't do it," and my hand trembled as it held her arm.

She smiled and said, "When I get up, you can do it, Grant," and freed her arm from my hand. She walked on. I stood there awkwardly between her and the two boys until she came to the bottom of the quarry wall and put her hands on it, as if to test it; then I backed up and joined them. They said nothing to me, did not look at me.

Dan said apprehensively to the air, "She shouldn't try it."

Freddie said, "She'll make it."

We all watched her begin. And from where we stood, it did not seem hard. Her body looked small against the cliffside, but lithe and sure as an animal's as it moved slowly up and to the right, perhaps six feet, then to the left and up, perhaps ten, then nearly straight up, one cautious arm stretching overhead to the next hold, one safe foot pulling slowly up to the ledge that the hand had just tried and abandoned. I saw that she was following, with perfect confidence, the possible path up that we had sketched in our minds. Now she was at a point nearly halfway up, where, for a considerable stretch that was almost horizontal, she could safely traverse by side-stepping, and there, for no reason but the challenge of it, she turned slowly and looked down at us and shouted, "Come on in, the water's fine."

Dan groaned a little and Freddie said, "Jesus!" and I

laughed with all the uneasiness that I felt. But already Milly
was facing the cliff wall again and, once more, starting up, left,
right, up, across, up again, slowly, slowly, and now I could not
help wondering that she had never done it before. She was
always the boldest of us—it was always she who climbed the
highest trees, dived first from the highest board, just as it was
she who ran fastest, who had made it almost a point to know
most about snakes and birds and the life of the woods and
water, who had the quickest judgment and the pluck at once
to act on it—and I found myself remembering a time when
Freddie's clothes caught fire from the blaze of a pile of leaves
we were burning, and, while Dan and I stood gaping, Milly
hurled herself at him and in a minute had rolled his heavier
body on the ground and put out the flame. Now that we were
older, she was still the best in nearly everything—swiftest at
tennis and with the deadliest serve; surest at the tiller; as accurate as two of us, at least, before a target, even though with
a borrowed gun; still boldest and best on a cliff.

She was almost at the top, moving cautiously across the last
steep drop, and then, with a sudden scramble that sent a small
shower of gravel bouncing down and off the face of stone, she
was over the slope where the treacherous cliff became innocent
field. She disappeared, and when she reappeared at a point
where the guardrail came close to the edge, she waved down,
cupped her hands to shout "Easy!" and stood there for a moment while the summer wind blew at her short, straight hair
which, in that morning sun, was white.

Dan and Freddie turned simultaneously and raced up the
gravel slope to meet her. Following them at a walk, I could
only hate myself—and hate that feeling more. The three were
halfway down again when I met them, and they were all laughing.

"Grant's turn now," Milly cried.

I laughed uncomfortably and said, "Oh, listen—"

She could not listen. "It's easy as anything. You'll see."

When we stood together again in the bottom of the quarry, Dan and Freddie just looked at me—Dan with curiosity, Freddie with something more. Milly looked merely expectant, and when I hesitated, she said, "Come on, Grant. You'll have to hurry, because I have to get back to keep those stupid appointments in the village."

"I have to, too," I said.

"Well, then, hurry."

"All right," I said, and I made my way through the brush and the pools to the naked wall. I stood where she had stood and looked up. The height was alarming, but I thought that I could see the way that she had taken, and I began the climb. At first it was easy, as easy as her climb had seemed to be. I went up even more slowly than she, even more cautiously, but now I had no doubt that I could do it, and when I came to the ledge halfway up, where Milly had turned, I felt safe, and it was at that point that I was sure of something else. I knew that in doing this thing that she had done and that Dan and Freddie would not do, I was separating myself from them in her feelings about us and that I could have her.

Now, perhaps with that thought, I miscalculated the wall that I was climbing. I went left, went right, and then went left again, and suddenly there was nowhere to go, neither up nor down, right nor left; I was caught. My hands clutched separate protrusions, my feet rested on separate, scanty ridges of rock, and I was at a point where I stood nearly straight—a hideous parodied crucifixion, nothing behind or below me but the violence of air.

Everything in me fell to pieces. My hands, clinging to rock, broke out in sweat, and I felt sweat drench my back, my loins. But this first physical sensation was followed by a sensation

(I use the word advisedly) of another kind—a spread of inward terror, a kind of seepage through my being that carried on its currents an absolute fright, purest, I confess, cowardice. Then, through the abysses of cringing, depraved feeling into which I was sinking, voices reached me, the voices of Milly, Freddie, and Dan, a chorus of agitation, shouting directions, I suppose, but no words penetrated my muffling fear, only a long, shrill wailing that lent to that fear a touch of simple, stupid melancholy. My hands were gripping rock with the total strength of my fingers, and then all of my body except my rigid hands began gently to tremble. It was only when the wet skin of my neck and back began to register the heat of the sun with a maddening, relentless prickling that my brain seemed once more to swim up out of the black terror that had swamped me, and told me to consider some action. With that, the trembling slowly stopped and I was able to look down at my feet to see if they could really not find some place to move. The ledge of rock on which my right foot was planted was larger than the ledge on which my left was, and I saw that it was just possible that I could get both my feet where my right foot was, and still balance myself by pushing against the bulge of rock to which my left hand clung. It was that or nothing, for I knew that I would not be able to get through another such fit of utter fright as had first overtaken me, but would certainly lose my grip. Well, I did it. I don't know, now, how I succeeded, how, once my two feet were together, I succeeded in pushing my hand away from the rock on the left, clutching the rock on my right, and getting my right foot back to the safe, wider ledge that I had left, and then the whole of myself. But I did, and once I was back there at the point from which I could move on up with reasonable safety, I stopped to rest, to recover.

I heard the excited voices below, but still there were no words. I had not yet escaped from that pit of abjectness, of

shrill and total demoralization into which I had plunged. (I
have never escaped from it; whenever I remember this experience, I am overcome first by the same awful fright, then
by the sweating and trembling, and finally by the shuddering
shame which had still to come.) Now my mind was active and,
although the rest of the climb seemed like pure horror to me,
I knew that I must attempt it and could manage if I must. So
presently I began again, up, up, almost like scaling some per-
versely made ladder, across to the right again, then up again,
and now so slowly, slowly that all my muscles began to ache
with the strain. But my fear and my cowardice were supporting
me in caution and calculated patience, and even now, when I
could look up and see the top and the blue of heaven at the
rim of the quarry like a prize I would win, I climbed with
maniacal concentration, until I was at the last danger point,
the narrow sloping brow of this brute of a wall. For a moment
I put my cheek against the warm stone, as if to caress it into
kindness, and let my tired, aching fingers stroke it, then wiped
my sweaty hands on my pants legs and with tense, prayerful
clutchings and pushings up, took the last six steps that brought
me to the slope of the field. Like Milly's, my final scramble to
safety sent a shower of gravel down into the depths, and the
thin, perilous sound the stones made as they bounced off stone
brought back, for a moment, my earlier fright. But I fell forward under the guardrail, on my stomach, and lay for a moment with my face in the dusty weeds, and simply breathed.
The wind blew over me and cooled me as it dried me, even as
I was trembling again. Then I heard sounds, and looked up
and saw that Milly was standing there, alone, and I got to my
feet slowly and smiled at her.

"Now we're equal," she said quietly.

"Yes," I answered, deep in the luxury of my relief, and for

a moment, we were. She smiled at me, and she seemed to soften, to melt into a new kind of candor, a wholly different response from any she had been in the habit of giving.

We stood looking at each other, smiling, until she said in a voice soft with invitation, "Grant, come here." But the moment was passing. Something else was taking the place of relief, a hot flood of shame.

"No, thanks," I said, and then I was looking at her with the simplest distaste. After a long moment, I looked past her to where Dan and Freddie were climbing up to us. Then I walked jerkily away to them, and my back was turned to her when she called, "That was wonderful climbing, the way you got out of that spot!"

"Good boy!" Dan cried.

"Champ-een," said Freddie with a friendly jeer.

And we started back to the lake. They babbled all the way, but I was hardly there, immersed in degradation.

At the lake, I left them and went home. My mother had reminded me that we were expecting a second cousin of mine from California, a girl named Margaret Linden who was a year older than I, and I was to be there early. She did not arrive until late in the afternoon, and I met her just before dinner. Because she was there, my father, at my mother's suggestion, made cocktails for all of us, although they were not in the habit of asking me to drink with them. Margaret was a striking girl, with black hair and a white, rather long face, narrow, tipped eyes, and a large, voracious mouth, and whether it was her presence or the cocktails that braced me, I don't know, but after dinner I felt marvelous, as though I had mastered my life and the world with it. Then I wanted to see Milly, feeling that I had left that day unfinished, and I excused myself for an hour.

Milly was alone with her stepmother and father. She looked

very pretty, for her hair had been attended to in preparation for her dance the next evening, and she was wearing a white tennis dress that showed her brown neck and arms, and her brown legs were bare, and she looked cool and composed. "Let's walk," I suggested when we were standing alone on the terrace.

We walked, as if from old habit, toward the orchard. All the way I could feel that new thing between us, dancing, pulling, and now and then our bare arms touched and set it quivering. I took her hand as we walked on the dark path, and when we entered the orchard, she said, "Why did you look at me that way this afternoon?"

"What way?" I asked, and put my arms around her and began to kiss her.

She pulled stiffly away. "No, no, no. Grant."

But I pulled her back to me and said, "Remember, we're equals," and then I kissed her. There was still something in her to be overcome, I don't know what kind of resistance it was beyond alarm, but it was there even when she no longer protested and let me, at last, have her.

When she stopped crying, I explained that I had promised my mother that I would be back early because of my cousin. Milly did not want to come with me, so I took her home.

My mother was winding the phonograph when I came in; Margaret was there, but my father was not, he had had to go to the village about her trunk. The phonograph played "I Want to Be Happy," and Mother made us highballs, and I danced with both of them, Margaret and my mother.

Next night, at Milly's dance, I had to be with Margaret a good deal of the time, since she was a stranger—seeing to her introductions, dancing with her when she was without a partner—and so it worked out that I had only one dance with Milly, and we went through that in difficult silence. She looked very pretty, although she was without interest in the party and therefore without animation. The dress that Miriam Moore had provided was too fluffy and feminine for Milly's sense of herself, if not for her age; something, certainly, was wrong with it, as something was wrong with us.

6

Margaret Linden stayed with us for a month, and her visit made another difference. The year between our ages did not seem to matter, but the two years between Margaret and Milly might almost as well have been twenty. Milly wanted to be younger and less of a woman than she was; Margaret wanted to be older and more of a woman, and worldly, besides. She smoked cigarettes in a long black holder and she played bridge with the kind of easy concentration that makes champions. Milly hated bridge and loved tennis, but Margaret had not even brought a racket. There was also the matter of the fifth person, a difficult problem at either tennis or bridge, and when, for example, I suggested that we all sail, Milly would point out that the boat was really too small and that she would stay at home. After a few days, I gave up trying to bring them together, and I necessarily spent my time with Margaret, and with one or two slightly older people whom my mother would invite around. Then, after Margaret left again, I tried to renew the relationship with Milly that we had just begun on the day of Margaret's arrival, but she pushed me away, this time very firmly. She said, briskly, "Let's forget that messy business and be what we are, friends."

I said, "All right, if that's what you want." I could say this honestly, for that excitement had given way to a new one, and when Milly said then, "Your cousin had a good time, didn't she?" I answered, "Yes. She's coming again next year."

She came almost as soon as the house had been opened, and stayed again for a month, and so again, Milly and Dan and Freddie managed without me. Again, I made a few efforts to bring Margaret into that circle, but even though Milly was older now and looked it, and could very well have met Margaret on her own ground, she was cold to her. It was the awkwardness of trying to bring Margaret into our friendship that showed me, for the first time, that our friendship had grown into a strange one.

That was the summer when everyone sang "Chloe" and "Blue Skies" and "Ain't She Sweet," and these songs beat out the tempo for the hot, troubled, purely physical thing that sprang up between my cousin and me, and exhausted itself, all in that month. Perhaps it was because I had no illusions as to who it was that played the stalker's role in this affair that it left me, after Margaret had gone again, so at odds with everything, myself included, as if this relationship that I had wanted and taken, had somehow, in fact, taken me. And I was left with an ill-tempered sense of being incapable of repossessing myself.

My relationship with the other three was never the same again. I was suffering from some *Ich-schmertz* that was still outside their experience, and even though this was the summer that we found we were no longer hunting for fishing bait on Saturday nights, clambering around on our hands and knees in the dirt of damp places with a flashlight, but were going to dances at the club instead, and that on Sunday mornings, instead of meeting at sunrise to begin our day on the lake or in the woods, were sleeping until noon and then meeting on the golf course, even though, that is to say, this was the summer that marked our movement over into adult pleasures, I was no longer *of* them, as I had so long been. The original, naïve intimacy of the other three had not changed, and that, plus my own un-ease, expelled me.

Milly was beautiful. The ragged blond hair of earlier years was now always groomed, and for the first time the charming contours of her face were allowed to stand wholly clear. Her forehead was low, her cheeks, under the high bones, rather hollowed out, her chin, fine and pointed and perhaps a little cruel, and her neck, round and slender and long. Summer made her brown, with a high, warm color in her cheeks, and her gray-blue eyes were vivid and startling in their contrast with that skin. Her mouth in repose was perhaps a little petulant, almost sullen, and yet it had the expression not so much of the spoiled child as of the badgered one. So, too, was her manner with almost all people except the three of us—abrupt, more than that, almost self-protectively rude, as it had been with Margaret Linden. Whatever it was that beset her mouth showed itself more clearly in her relationship with us, and I knew now that we were no longer so much her friends as we were the indispensable props to something that appeared to be vanity and may have been, but was also, certainly, something much more.

Freddie and Dan went on in what was apparently the old way, making up with a doubled devotion, perhaps, for my lapse. I dropped more and more away from them, and after a while, as that summer drew on, seeing them together, seeing that intimacy still hold that should long before have altered its character or been abandoned entirely, and trying myself occasionally with awkward unsuccess to renew it, I could not be very sorry.

That year I finished school, and because our relationship had trailed off into the false thing that it had become for me, it was as well that I did not have a chance to go to Silverton the next summer. My mother had offered me her companionship in a trip abroad as a graduation gift. My father went to the country alone for the latter part of that summer, and when my mother and I came back from Europe after Labor Day, we went up to Silverton for a week end in order to close the house after his use of it.

Late in the first afternoon I walked over to the Fords' house and found that it was already closed for the winter. That iron deer stood in cool shadows, head lifted as if to sniff the rain that was coming, and I walked on over to the Moores' house. That, too, was already locked up, the shutters nailed tight, the doors boarded over. I stood on the terrace that lay above the lake and watched the sky darken. Far away in the valley hills, thunder rumbled and gurgled, and the wind that came ahead of the rain ruffled the dark water as though it had a surface of indigo feathers. The empty lake and the blackening landscape made me yearn, suddenly, to see them again, and the desultory chirpings of a few birds in those elms where they sometimes gathered in singing droves brought back, like a gasp, the emotions of the past. How frightfully desirable all that seemed! I could, I suppose, have driven to the village and probably found Freddie there, but it was not Freddie whom I wished to see —it was chiefly Milly, and after her, Dan. The wind blew at me. Trees were beginning to rock, waves to roll, long grass to lean. The thunder was much closer, sounding, in those hills, like a lot of boards being dropped one on top of the other in quick succession. I was consumed with regret: I wanted the past again with a wild hunger, I wanted to live it over more blithely. And I said, How foolish!

That was late in 1929. I knew as well as anyone that you cannot have the past again, in any year, but I did not know that I was never again to come back to Silverton. And yet, of course, you always do have the past, and I did not know this either—you always do have the past in the sense that it has already settled your future in some degree, and probably, to that degree, spoiled it.

TWO

Winters in the City,
Older

1

A windy, wintry tunnel of a crosstown street in the West Forties. A small hand in a tautly drawn white kid glove on my sleeve. I turned. A veiled face that was laughing. Snow blew desultorily between this face and mine. "Grant Norman?"

It was Milly Moore.

"I saw you from my cab, and I knew at once—I couldn't have been wrong! Darling, get in there with me out of this wind."

The driver had double-parked and the door of his cab stood open. "Milly. Good God."

"Darling, get in!"

"I can't. I'm late for an appointment. Right here. But look—"

"Grant?"

"When can I see you?"

Horns were blasting impatiently. The cab driver tapped out a quick summons to Milly.

"Do you live in New York?"

"Yes."

"Are you in the book?"

"Yes."

"Darling, I'll call you."

One more long glance through the spotted veil, with the filthy city wind blowing gray snow down at us, and, "Darling Grant! This is wonderful!" Then she ran.

"Milly! Wait!" I called, but she had gone. I watched her

slim ankles above the steep black calfskin heels, and then I
watched the cab pull away and saw the gloved hand lifted at
the smirched window. It was over.

Had it happened at all, I wondered as I bought the newspaper that I had stopped for, and was pushed and shoved by
less visionary comrades. I knew quite well what day it was, and
what year, and yet my eye settled, as if for confirmation, not
on the headline of the paper that I held, but on *January 10,
1938*. Snowflakes fell on the paper and left marks like those of
tears.

Milly did not telephone me. She wrote, instead, a note that
came next day to my Tenth Street walk-up. If she had telephoned, she might have prepared me for those developments
of which I was still ignorant, but her note told me nothing
that was new and too much of what was old. *If you honestly
want to see us, Grant, come for dinner on Friday*, it said. *It's
against the law to hunt birds' eggs in the Park, and it's winter
besides, but there are other ways in which we can recall for an
evening at least that time which only you, apparently, have been
willing to forget. Come at seven-thirty*. The note was signed
simply *Milly*, and there was an engraved address at the top of
the sheet—a Fifth Avenue number in the Eighties. The business of the birds' eggs I found rather chilling, and it was that
about which I wondered rather than about identities—to
whom the plural might refer, for example; I simply assumed,
foolishly, that Gregory Moore and his wife were now in New
York and that Milly lived with them. My keeping her thus
enclosed in the situation of her youth may have shown as much
about my relationship to the past as her note showed about
hers.

Friday was the next day. The address was for one of those
monstrously solid granite apartment buildings with a gilded

grilled entrance meant to suggest a palace of marble. I asked
the doorman for the Moores' apartment, and was told that
there were no Moores. I pulled out Milly's note to ascertain the
address and I showed it to him.

"There is Mrs. Ford, whose name *was* Moore. Do you want
Mrs. Daniel Ford?"

He had everything all mixed up, I thought impatiently,
before the jolt of the fact struck me, and then, "Of course," I
said, and managed through my shock weakly to add, "I forgot."

He gave an order, and the elevator boy stiffened for me
and pulled back the door.

Should I have known? Why? I had nearly forgotten them
in my own concerns. As we had moved apart, so had our worlds,
and now, as the elevator lifted me up to them with velvet swift-
ness, that gap of worlds seemed to stretch almost frighteningly
wider. Who were they now? And who, for that matter, was
I? I had no desire to account for myself to them, to tell them
how, after my mother's death, I had, for example, spent my
nights in fifty-cent hotels, or how, after my father's death,
which came first, I followed my mother west and became the
hovering, incompetent, and unwilling protector of her poverty.

At Christmas, in 1929, my father's gift to my mother was
a bottle of bootlegged Scotch which she discovered only after
the janitor in his office building had called the police who
in turn had called on her to say that my father had gone down
there that morning to blow out his brains. Everything was
lost, and the house on Waverly Place, like the house in Silverton, and the contents of both, were not even ours to sell. I
had been enrolled in a New England university and I managed
to finish out the term, but by the end of it, my mother, as if

searching for her home, had already gone to California with little more than a trunk of clothes and an inadequate annuity. In February, I followed in a day coach.

She had no relatives to speak of there, only a distant cousin or two by that time, and no real friends any longer, but San Francisco seemed to promise her some refuge after the savage reversals of New York. Yet when I arrived, I found her already disappointed, lonely and querulous in a small apartment on Russian Hill where she sat staring out of her large window at the usual items—the bay, the Embarcadero, a piece of bridge, Alcatraz. There was no room for me and she had of course hardly enough money for herself.

I enrolled at the University and lived in Berkeley, hashing in a sorority house and sleeping and studying in a basement room in a tennis club where, in exchange for the room, I acted as night watchman and where, too, when I was lucky, I picked up a child or two on the courts as a pupil. They were difficult, threadbare years, and I was glad when they were over, even though the best that I could manage then was a job as copy boy on a San Francisco newspaper. Everyone on the paper was expected to learn to write in a cozy tone of heavily domestic irony that I never quite managed in the small assignments that began to come to me, and the political views of the owners and the editor, maintained with a Parnassian detachment from the realities of 1933 and 1934, constantly irritated me. After eighteen months, I was let go, and at almost exactly that moment, my mother let go. Night after night, sitting in her small and by now rather shabby prison, a ruined old woman not yet fifty, she stared out at the lights of that other, larger prison, until one night when fog blurred the city and no lights seemed to belong to objects or even to represent them, she emptied a bottle of whisky and took enough nembutal to put an end to her pointless vigil. I found her the next afternoon in her chair, with her hands open, the palms cupped a little, as though she were begging for something.

Now came the fierce time for me, when I did beg, until, after six months of nothing, I found a job on a union paper that I suited and that suited me. My life slipped another notch as it was drawn closely into the tough intrigues of the water front, but out of this experience I was able to write occasional reports on west coast labor that found their way into liberal periodicals in New York, and these reports brought me, finally, an offer from one of these periodicals, *The New World*, to come to New York as a staff writer. I had been there a little less than a year, and now, as I stepped from that elevator into the foyer at which it stopped, I felt as much a stranger to my-self as whatever life lay beyond it had become a stranger—alien, as when a child, staring into a mirror, suddenly sees him-self there as someone else, an imperturbable interloper, a stranger in his place. It had been a long time since I had felt such a deep, detached sense of my life's not being in the least my own. I looked at my gloved hand as it hovered over the but-ton that would ring a bell inside and admit me, and my hand was like some totally unfamiliar object. Then of itself it plunged, and almost at once the door flew open and I was en-gulfed in arms.

Milly's arms, around my neck, were bare and perfumed, and I was looking down into her blue eyes, dazzled with tears. The heavy, man's arm that was around my shoulder and the hand that was thumping me were Freddie Grabhorn's, and to look at him, I had to lift my eyes. He was half a head taller than I, as Milly was half a head shorter. They were both talking and laughing, and I was laughing, and for a moment everything was confusion as we stood there enclosed in that senselessly babbling embrace. Then all arms abruptly dropped and we stood separate, smiling, before closed doors, and I knew that I had, through this welcome, been returned to myself.

Milly's smile faded as she put her hand on a great, ornamental knob. "Before we go in, Grant—I have to tell you this. Be careful of what you say when Dan is with us."

"Of what I say?" I was still smiling.

"It's important, Grant, that you—" Freddie began with an expression of utmost solemnity, but Milly broke into his speech.

"Let's not stand out here any longer. Come in. We'll explain." She opened the door and we entered the generous vestibule of the apartment. There, among tapestries and large mirrors with heavy, rococo frames, Freddie took my hat and coat.

"What's wrong with Dan?" I asked then.

Milly's voice was hushed now. "He's so easily upset. Ever since his parents—ever since that terrible accident—it's been very difficult. . . ."

"You know, Milly, I'm absolutely ignorant. I've been three thousand miles away from all of you, and for almost ten years. I didn't know you were married. You'll have to start at the beginning." I had answered in a whisper, too.

Then Freddie whispered, "Unpleasant things upset him. He's likely to go to pieces when he's reminded. . . . Any kind of violence. . . . You've got to remember that anything unpleasant at all may remind him."

Milly was looking at me intently, Freddie was looking at me severely, and I did not yet understand at all why both of them spoke with that portentous quality in their secretive voices, or why, indeed, I should suddenly have found myself the center of that hushed conspiracy in the vestibule. But their lives, I was to learn soon enough, were lived in an atmosphere of intrigue, and not only the intrigue that attaches to Dan's business, oh no, not only that. Had it been only that, there would be no story for me to tell.

"The beginning . . ." Milly was murmuring vaguely. "You didn't know we were married, Grant? Yes, we must start at the beginning, if we can." She seemed unable to be more definite, and looked at me with a helpless lifting of the eyes and a kind of plea in the sudden sharp elevation of her hands. Then, smiling brilliantly, "Oh, but it's good to see you!" she cried in her friendly voice, and seized my arm. "Darling, come in!"

And then, after all that, Dan was not there.

It came to me that I had never seen Milly outside a country setting, that she had always been that free and striving creature of the summer, and that as I had known her, there was almost nothing that would have promised this. She stood before me in a long black gown of perfect severity except that the deep neckline transformed itself into a tall rolled satin collar that suggested the corolla of a calla lily if one could imagine a black calla, and from this rose her throat and lovely head, with the fair hair pulled severely up and back and fastened in the simplest twist, a housewife's bun, where she wore a blue flower. Her beauty had grown, somehow, to exist in its calm, when she was calm, a development that one would no more have predicted than one would have predicted that she should have chosen such an establishment as we were now in as proper to her.

This drawing room was huge without being spacious, two floors in height but with great, heavy beams on its ceiling that oppressively reduced that height; walls covered in walnut paneling on which hung, with a cold and somehow cluttered air, eighteenth-century British portraits of bland dignitaries and dim, damask beauties; the whole full of walnut furniture, especially, it seemed, sidepieces, and doorways full of heavy draperies, and a towering fireplace that was all carving, and floors covered with oriental ostentation, and here and there, great stuffed ottomans squatting like the plump potentates that they must once have been made for. Then immediately it occurred to me: of course, the elder Fords. The little pharaoh and his sister-consort. I stood in the ambience not of Milly Moore but of Bianca Ford, and it was not only easy but really inevitable to imagine this room peopled with those small, important, comically regal beings—Bianca in her robes and large jewels holding court from one of those ottomans, he, in a maroon shirt under a navy blue jacket, leaning against one of those sidepieces and lecturing cryptically on a Raeburn opposite, his Edwardian beard moving precisely with his mouth. It truly was the past in which we stood.

We? There stood Freddie. There stood Freddie looking at me with fond suspicion in his flicking, hazel eyes. He was both heavier and taller than I should have expected him to be. His broad-boned face had filled out, and its skin gleamed with a kind of polish. He wore a dark blue suit with considerably padded shoulders, expensively tailored but rather theatrical, a little ineptly vain, I could not help thinking, in the attention that had gone to its lines and what they were to imply about the body that it clothed. His brown hair was lighter than I remembered and wavier, but perhaps that latter effect arose from its meticulous grooming. There was nothing gentle about his face, yet it was soft, almost pampered, certainly sleek; and as, in that moment, I looked at him, certain kinds of work leapt to my mind: he might have been the manager of a fashionable small hotel, or he might have been a man who sold boats behind a great plate glass window on Park Avenue.

"The beginning," he was saying. "How far back is that?"

"Grant, sit down," Milly urged, and took my arm again. We sat side by side on an enormous sofa.

"Christmas, 1929," I said.

"Most of the fill-in can wait for Dan," Freddie said with crisp authority, "but we have to tell you about him before he comes."

"Where is Dan?"

"He'll be down soon," Freddie went on. "He came in late. He had a fracas at the gallery today—someone questioning his judgment on the authenticity of a certain picture. He was all torn up. Milly made him lie down."

All the time I had felt Milly's eyes upon me, and I was aware of the gentle rise and fall of her breasts with her breathing. I turned to her and was startled by the happiness in her face, so that I laughed. "Gallery, Milly?" I asked. "Do you mean The Ford Gallery?"

"It's his now," she said. "After his parents' death, it went to him."

"They're dead?"

"The accident I spoke of. It happened almost four years ago. On the day of Dan's graduation. It nearly killed him, too."

Freddie said, "Milly saved him."

"How?" I asked stupidly.

Milly spoke again. "Remember what Dan was like as a boy, Grant. You do remember, don't you? How sensitive? Different from the rest of us? Don't you remember?"

"Ye-es," I allowed her, but thinking that there seemed now to be two Millies, this one who had just spoken, the urgent, distraught, intense Milly whose hands were clasped tight, and the calm, easy one who had embraced me five minutes before and carelessly called me darling half the time.

"You remember—he couldn't ever bear to see anything hurt. How he shot. Only at targets. I used to have to bait his hook for him when we used live bait. Minnows. Really, he

didn't ever like to fish. Just as he hated it when everything between us was not at peace?"

"Yes," I allowed again, and as I glanced up at Freddie I
had a sense of him as the custodian of an experimental process.

"Sensitive beyond the norm, perhaps, to cruelty and pain.
No curiosity in that direction—"

It was a portrait not without its truth, yet surely the truth
was partial. I remembered that both Milly and Freddie had
had an almost coldly scientific interest in cruelty and pain in
which Dan did not share. When birds were struck with stones,
he did wince and sigh while they moved closer; there was that
butterfly and beetle collection, for which he did only the print-
ing; there were certain messy experiments in vivisection on
frogs, conducted when he was not present, and that business of
blowing a frog up with a straw stuck into him that every country boy enjoys. The strong wish for peace and the naïve
maneuvers toward it—yes certainly; but minnows, and the
whole implied excess of tenderness?

"And then, to him! That dreadful accident. Well. Don't
you see? Darling?" It was as if she had been struggling for her
point, and then, having made it, allowed herself to relax in that
last word. Everything softened in it and she was looking at me
with kind, candid eyes.

"You haven't told me," I said. "Except that, I gather, his
parents were killed? I don't mean to be stupid."

She laughed. It was again the clear, welcoming laugh, absolutely open, and she said, "You're not stupid!" with the blunt-
ness of a child. It might have been the girl, Milly, who had
spoken, and I said something like that, and she laughed again
with her peculiar note of happiness, careless laughter.

But Freddie was solemn as he still stood there, above us,
outside our sudden pleasure. He wished to take us out of it, it
seemed, for he said, "Yes, Grant, you have to think of it as hap-

pening to *him*. To Dan, mind you. Not to you, not to me. We'd have taken it differently. But to *him*." The whispered pronoun lingered on the air.

Milly was looking up at him and permitted herself to say, "Yes," as though this were indeed a permission, and with that, Freddie went on. "Let me tell you quickly now. He'll be down."

"Yes. Please do."

"You see, his mother and father had driven up to New Haven early that morning for the ceremonies, and then they were going to drive on to Silverton with Dan for the summer. Mr. Ford knew some short cuts. Country roads. He was driving an open car. Too fast. In the twilight he missed a turn. Dan was thrown clear of the car and, by some miracle, wasn't even scratched. Stunned, but not hurt. He picked himself up and heard moans—and then, screams. The motor was still running. He reached in there, over their trapped bodies, and turned off the ignition. They were pinned in, mangled and pinned in and completely conscious. It was a lonely road. No cars. In his frenzy, he tried to lift the car. Hopeless, of course. Then he started to run for help. In one direction, then back and in the other direction, then back again. This went on—for twenty minutes, thirty minutes. Finally, by the time someone came, they had died. But only after these most awful agonies—vocal, you understand. Conscious. And something died in Dan. To have to watch that, to have to listen to that—if you were Dan!"

"Do you see, Grant?" Milly asked softly.

"Oh, I do see," I said, and I did, in the fullest horror, but not only because Dan was that particularly sensitive person they had drawn for me—even more because of the particular relation, that accepted equality, that he enjoyed with those people, his parents. It was the shock of his grief, his lonely sense of loss, that I could most easily grasp rather than that other shock that seemed most to concern them, and of which, I felt, they were determined to persuade me. That persuasion I resisted, perhaps, in determining that now I would be cool, and so I asked only, "When did that happen? You said—?"

"June, 1934."

"And then you were married?"

"Oh, not then!" Milly said quickly. "After the accident, Dan was in a sanitarium for a long time, you know, Grant, and—"

"A sanitarium?"

Freddie broke in. "But of course. He was a ruin, I tell you, Grant, a ruin."

"Ah, yes."

"A complete breakdown," said Milly.

"And then?"

"Then the sanitarium released him to me only on condition—"

"To you? But why?"

She looked at me for a long sad moment. "Who else did he have but Freddie and me?"

I looked back at her and said, "You see, I am stupid," and she shook her head impatiently and said, "No, no. Of course, you couldn't understand, having been away from it all. You see, he had the bodies brought to Silverton and they were buried there, but my father persuaded him not to live in his parents' house, to come to ours instead. He did. But it was only for a few weeks. He was—"

"He was ruined," Freddie said, "he was just ruined."

But Milly took up again, that second, urgent Milly. "My father persuaded him that he should go to the sanitarium. He was there for—"

I wanted them to go more slowly, and I said, "What sanitarium?"

"An excellent place called Windhaven." From firm Freddie.

"Near Silverton?"

"No, no. Long Island."

"Oh, yes. And then?"

"Milly started to tell you, Grant."

"Yes. I'm sorry."

"His doctor released him with the understanding that he be sheltered from shock. Especially from any needless experience of suffering. Or violence. That was to be expected. Of course. That is what we have been trying to say, Grant. From the moment you came in. So, darling, do mind what you say, won't you?" In that single speech, she had changed again, from the coldly intense to the calm and warm. Her skin was very white, with an almost ivory pallor and glow, and her gray-blue eyes looked at me with a perfectly friendly plea.

Again I stiffened to reject that persuasion, which one would have found it so easy to accede to. I said, "And *then* you were married?"

"Quite soon. He came back here. Reopened this apartment. His parents', of course—"

I interrupted her again. "But doesn't *this* remind him all the time?" and I indicated the crowded, heavily archaic room we were in.

"He needs *some* mooring," Freddie said.

"It's the apartment he's always known," said Milly. "And we didn't really think much of this, when he was—out, again."

"Perhaps this place *is* bad for him," Freddie said.

"He seemed so well by then, and Freddie did need him—"

"Freddie?"

"At the gallery," Freddie said.

"The gallery," said I.

"But, of course, he doesn't know that either, Freddie. How

could he? Dan's father sent Freddie to college, Grant, and
Freddie studied the fine arts, too—like Dan. Then, when he
finished, which was a year before Dan, Mr. Ford took him into
the gallery as an assistant, a runner; and as it worked out, you
see, when the Fords were dead, and Dan was ill, there was,
naturally, only Freddie to manage."

"Oh, yes. Naturally. And now?"

"Now Freddie works with Dan."

I laughed. "How really nice for you, Freddie!"

He harrumphed a bit and said, "It works out well," and I
smiled at him.

Milly cried, "And for Dan! Freddie's marvelous at it!"

"I'm sure he is."

"Here's Dan, here he is now, and now we'll talk about you,
Grant."

A door was closing on the claustral balcony that stretched
across one end of that huge room, and Dan came quickly down
the shadowy flight of stairs that brought him to our level, and
then, with his arms out, quickly down the length of the room,
saying, "Grant." He seized my shoulders and we looked at one
another. Whatever I had felt until now, even for Milly, had
been tentative, but in Dan's presence, all my earliest affections
spilled warmly through me, and, holding his arms as he held
my shoulders, I said, "Ah, Dan!" in a shaken voice.

"Grant, how good, how good!" he exclaimed.

Then again there was a kind of babble, as there had been
in the foyer, and the four of us stood close together, and then
Dan stepped back a little and Freddie laid his arm over Dan's
shoulders in a brotherly fashion, and Milly, too, had moved
with them, and stood on Dan's other side, so that what had
been our momentary, exclaiming intermixture had suddenly become an arrangement, even a formation, the three of them

standing together, I before them and apart, and Milly saying.
"How do we look to you, Grant?"

In such apparent accidents lie our premonitions, were we
but sensible enough to read them, as, certainly, there I was not.
I simply said, surveying them, "Freddie's put on weight, but it
gives him a prosperous air."

"Don't remind me," he said.

"Milly's the most beautiful woman I've seen in this town."

"Darling!"

"And Dan"—I let my eyes rest affectionately on his beautiful face—"Dan—"

"Yes?"

"Why, you look fine, simply fine!"

"I'll light the fire," Freddie said. "It's not really warm in
here, is it?" He turned away and struck a match to the logs
that lay on the enormous hearth.

"And a drink," Milly said. "Many drinks. Because we're all
together again." She stepped to a recess beside the chimney
and pulled at a bell rope, and in a moment a servant appeared
with a cocktail tray. This was deposited on a table that, oddly
enough, was moved before Freddie's chair, and my surprise
must have shown itself, for Dan, who stood looking on, said,
"Freddie's our bartender, Grant—when we can get him."

"Oh, yes."

"Martinis?" Freddie asked, and then, with an air of execu-
tive authority that was proper, I should have thought, to the
master of the household alone, he began mixing them.

"You people see a good deal of each other," I said.

"Of course!" Milly cried. "After all, darling, only you were
unfaithful."

I started. "That's a strong word."

"Is there any other that's better?"

"Well—"

"Darling, what did become of that girl?"

"Girl?"

"That Margaret."

"Margaret."

"Your cousin!"

"Oh. Why— Good heavens, Milly, do you remember her? That ended in the summer that it began."

"Did it?" Milly asked without laughter, and there was no word from the others.

I found myself stumbling through an explanation. "It was the next summer, I think, that she married. She married a middle-aged Swede. She's lived in Stockholm ever since."

"Has she?" Milly had gone miles away from me.

"Can't we sit down?" Dan asked.

Of the three of them, Dan had changed least. He looked exactly as he should have looked: like a young and successful dealer in fine things. I watched him as he crossed to that sofa where Milly had seated herself again, and now the two of them sat as, a little while before, Milly and I had sat. If the accident in which his parents had been killed had had any terrible effects, they were not visible in his walk, his carriage, or his face. He still looked like the youngest of us, with dark, bright, expectant eyes, and an air, generally, that suggested anticipation. His hair was cut as it had been for as far back as I could remember— short, like a thick cap of clipped fur, the hairline rounded over his forehead, dipping in a little at his temples. His complexion was dark and he had that deep color in his cheekbones, and the mole was still beside his nose. He was a man now, of course, not a boy, but I could hardly have believed it if, in the lamplight that shone on his head, I had not seen a fragmentary glint of silver here and there among the dark bristle on the side of his head. Later, too, I was to notice the difference in his voice,

but now I could only say again, "Dan, you look fine, really
fine."

"We want to hear about you now, Grant," Freddie said, as
he began to serve us his Martinis. And he said this abruptly, as
though he suspected some intention in my remark that he
was determined to deflect.

"Me?" I asked. "It's the most common story. I am De-
pression's Child." Although I said that flippantly, I felt an inward shudder. They had been brutalizing years, I knew, in
which more had been lost than gained, but I could not count
the toll, only register it in such a shock as this, for example,
with which I felt my difference now from these other three.
In the overstuffed and overpaneled and overheated room in
which we sat, with firelight dancing on their expensive and expectant faces, I let myself imagine that what they held were
not cocktails but great orbs of palest topaz cut for crystal
chalices, some fantasy of treasure and of fortune that had the
effect, in turn, of making me feel slightly seedy, even of remind-
ing me that I was well overdue for a haircut. I drank quickly
from what, in my hands, was indubitably a Martini, the finest.

"We knew that your mother went west, and that you were
there, in college," Milly said. "But tell about it."

I started to tell about my mother's death, but Freddie, with
some sharp intuition of the disaster that I was about to recount,
perhaps simply from the tenses of my verbs, deflected me again.
It was about the newspaper job that he wished to know, and
I allowed the deflection, but when I came to my union work,
and began to tell them an anecdote about police violence in
a water-front lockout, he steered me away again and asked
abruptly how long I had been in New York. It was all very
expertly done, and although it was made moderately easy for
him by the fact that he was constantly moving among us, in
and out of the conversation with his Martini pitcher, his new

cocktails and his pourings that would seem to draw him out
of the talk for a moment and allow him to enter it abruptly at
a tangent when he came back in, I could not help admiring his
skill and I was never deceived into thinking that he had, at any
point, withdrawn. But what a nerve-wracking task he had taken
upon himself! I could feel his presence, its sharp, collected
awareness, ready to spring at any point whenever I was talking,
and I could feel him relax when I turned the questioning back
to Milly or to Dan.

I asked her, for example, about Gregory and Miriam Moore,
and for the few moments that she answered, Freddie even left
the room. "They're still there," she said, "in Albany. Engrossed.
It really was truest love. How I hated it!" And her brothers?
One, it seemed, was in her father's office, the other in a Wall
Street brokerage firm. She seldom saw them. Then it seemed
positively crude not to murmur something, if only the most
cursory expression of sympathy, to Dan, about his tragedy, and
so I tried. Milly took his hand in a spontaneous gesture of
communion and protection and he asked wanly, "You
knew?"

And then Freddie, who had come quietly back into the
room, said briskly, "But tell us, Grant, what are you doing
here?"

The question startled me. For a moment, with my sense of
being a stranger, I thought that he must mean there in that
room, with them, and I said, "Here? Why—"

"Here in New York."

"Oh, yes. But haven't I told you that?"

"No, you haven't. Not a word."

Milly said, "Another cocktail, Freddie dear, please," and
Freddie busied himself again with his bottles, his ice, his pitcher.
Now I saw that Dan had fallen into a funk of grief, a reverie
remote from us, his eyes glazed over as he remembered them,

and I said, "It's not very interesting work. Not half as interesting as yours must be."

"But, Grant, interesting or not, we want to know," Milly said, and glanced sidewise, apprehensively, at Dan.

Freddie, starting up with his pitcher, said, "Of course, we do." He began to fill Milly's glass, which was nearly full.

"Not for me, Freddie," she said. "For Dan, for Grant, and you."

He filled Dan's glass and Milly took it and put it in Dan's hand. He sipped at it, and that film lifted from his eyes.

"Not for me, thanks," I said, and Freddie filled his glass again, and they were all looking at me.

"Well, you don't read *The New World*, I gather."

"No, why?" Milly asked.

"I'm on the staff there."

"Oh. Well, that's interesting, isn't it?"

"For me, yes. But I'd guess it's pretty far away from what interests you."

Dan had said very little. Now he spoke. "That's the magazine for which Drucquer does the art."

"No," I said. "He's on *World Progress*. They're much alike, I suppose." They were not alike, of course, except in their appearance, and it seemed astonishing that Dan should be so distant from both that he would not know which critic of painting was associated with each. But he seemed hardly to notice my correction.

"Drucquer," he was saying with a quaver. "An ignorant man."

"Is he? I wouldn't know. I'm not up on painting. I read him occasionally, that's all."

"Drucquer."

"Drucquer," Freddie broke in. "He's typical. There's only about one civilized art critic in this town. Just about one who writes out of real knowledge and feeling and a wide view of art as a whole. But the place is full of the Drucquers! The little dogmatic impressionists. Sometimes I think that I could do better."

"Why don't you try, Freddie?" I asked.

"I've been tempted."

"Drucquer," Dan said again, doggedly, as if speaking out of a stupor. "Drucquer."

And Milly cried, half in agitation, half in gaiety, it was hard to know which, "Oh, darling, Dan, dear, forget him, he doesn't *matter!*"

I watched Milly. It was fascinating to watch her. She was holding both his hands, those beautiful hands that had already made me think that he ought to make things, not to sell them. She held them, stubby brown hands with short fingers and broad, impeccable nails, in her white hands, plied them and pressed them, and urged him, with such sisterly solicitation, to please forget all that, that again I had the notion that here there was an excess, I did not quite know of what, but surely an excess. Now she was all the first Milly, the calm, possessed Milly who used endearments without thinking of them as endearments, the dear, darling, how-lovely Milly, all easy, all understanding, all—as I then began to see—all loving, and all untouched.

"Drucquer," Dan said again. "I can't be asked to meet that kind of opinion. The thing is, Grant, you see—"

It was now that I knew that there had been a change in him. I did not know how deep that change was, and certainly I did not know the sources of it (I was unwilling to believe entirely in *their* explanations), but there had been a change, that I did know. He spoke with an odd querulousness, in an almost petulant voice like that of a spoiled child—he who had never been spoiled, only always beatified. I groaned for him.

"You see, we have this new Van Gogh. An early work, apparently. We acquired it very recently, and last month we showed it." He hesitated. "Or do you know?" he asked suddenly.

"No, I don't know. I haven't followed art news. Now I will. Go on, Dan."

He gave me a stricken look. Milly's hands rubbed his. Her eyes widened and narrowed at me. She said, "This is so silly. Freddie, for heaven's sake, a drink."

Freddie had rather sunk down in his tapestried chair. He roused himself and looked owlishly at all our glasses. Dan's was empty, and Freddie's own was empty, and once more he poured the ice water from his pitcher, dropped in new ice, measured with precision, slowly stirred, and moved among us. As he poured another cocktail for Dan and another for himself, Dan's voice started up again.

"This Drucquer. He published a thing on the show a few weeks back. You didn't see it?"

"No," I said.

"And I wrote him. And today he came in. And he wanted to argue."

I had been watching Milly, who looked depressed and beautiful, and for the moment that Dan spoke, I had closed my eyes, so that I only heard him, did not see him. The voice was like that of a superannuated invalid discoursing on his ailments. I opened my eyes again and saw that he had got his hands out of Milly's, and they were fluttering before him in a foolish, ineffective way. I was about to leap up and say something directly to him, something that would bring him back to me, and to himself, when Milly took up the new cocktail and tried to put it in his hand.

"Darling, it's so unimportant," she implored him.

"Oh, I suppose so," he agreed, and let his hands fall on his

legs, but I did not feel that he was relaxing so much as letting
something fall inside himself as his hands fell outside, letting
something go.

Impressions had come too fast that evening, and they were
all undefined, but through them all was the dominant impression of uneasiness, of Freddie watching, of Milly shifting back
and forth from candor to some concealed complicity, of Dan,
in spite of his appearance and first easy friendliness, living in
some dark distress or deep indifference. But see how confused
and vague even this impression was—distress or indifference?
It could hardly have been both, or so I thought. And Freddie
had ceased to watch at just the moment that Dan was most
distressed, had fallen, then, into a kind of drunken indifference
of his own.

The drinking, and Milly's encouragement of it, had impressed me, too, and as we moved now into another darkly
paneled, heavily beamed room to dine, I could not fail to observe that Milly and I were nearly sober, and that Freddie and
Dan, if not quite drunk, were certainly not sober. There was
wine at dinner, and the effect on the two was different. Conversation turned almost at once to childhood and Silverton,
and the wine, together with Milly's animated recollections,
brought out in Dan something of his old animation, a dance of
laughter in his eyes, the light breathiness into his voice. Freddie seemed content simply to be there, and sat in heavy silence
as he emptied glass after glass of wine.

We were sitting at the middle of a long table. At the empty
ends were thickly clustered candles and large blue hydrangea
plants in silver bowls. Freddie and I sat side by side, and opposite us, side by side, sat Milly and Dan. It was that old pattern of the senior Fords, and as I looked across the table, I had
a strong conviction that here again I beheld the relationship
of Dan's parents, or part of it—the brother-sister fondness and

equality, the imperviousness to passion. What was missing was
the eccentricity, the vast security, the comic superiority. And
a child across from them to share in it all. Instead, they had
me, they had Freddie. And yet, as I laughed and chatted with
them over events that were stone dead to me, their pleasure in
recollection warmed me. Quite simply, I loved them.

Freddie may have been listening or he may not have been.
I glanced at him occasionally and saw him perfectly solemn,
perfectly happy, and once he turned to me and his light eyes
were filled with perfect benignity. "Come often," he managed.
Could I have been as mistaken in him as that muttered invitation made me feel?

After dinner, over brandy, Dan suggested music, and we
listened to a lot of recordings of Scarlatti. The thin, rigid patterns of sound could not fill that room, which required more
than the little sonatas of Scarlatti—the late Beethoven, at
least—but something in the very smallness of the music was
soothing to all of us, or so I felt, and as those fugal airs ran up
and down, with their precise grace and absolutely controlled
charm, I felt myself sink into a deeper happiness than I had
known for a long time. Dan and Freddie drank a good deal of
that brandy. I did not and Milly did not. I did not need to.
What I felt inside me was warmer than any benefit of liquor
could have been. And then, through all of that florilegium, *Le
Donne di Buon Umore*, I sat looking at Milly's profile. The
proud head was lifted alertly above that foil of high black
collar as she listened, and the music seemed like an adornment
to her, and as I let myself reflect in happy idleness on their like-
ness, the kind of beauty in the music and the kind of beauty in
her face—the composure that suggested not struggle but inter-
play between its own small elements which did not include
passion, passion that makes struggle and makes large elements
and makes composure great—and from that, on those two

Millies, this calm, friendly one who listened to Scarlatti now with the three of us, and that other, almost cold one who, over her cocktail, had remembered my cousin Margaret whom I had nearly forgotten—with this, my mind at last organized at least something from all that welter of unsettled impression which had been this evening.

It struck me that Milly belonged to both these men and yet belonged to neither. Or perhaps I should say that she had taken to herself qualities of each of these men, possessed herself of them by a kind of moral osmosis. The first Milly, who was without guile, was Dan's Milly; the other one, who was tensely cold, was Freddie's; and neither was a woman. The first was a more gracious version of a part of the child that she had been. The second was a frightened creature who had fled outside the limits of her sex and was thereby also another version of another part of the child that she had been. And thus I faced an irresistible conclusion: there was still a third Milly, Milly herself, a potential woman, more tender, more beautiful, who needed only to be found to be awakened; and she was mine.

The discovery was thrilling, like new knowledge, when, in a moment, we are taking a felt step beyond what we have been, and I was suddenly alive with that knowledge, vibrant as taut wires in a wind. Some wilder music than Scarlatti's sang up and down in my blood, some sharper, more stinging wine of happiness than that flood of youthful love that overtook me at dinner. And for the moment I was completely outside speculation, either as to the practical steps by which the goal of this knowledge was to be attained, or as to the difficulties, moral difficulties among them, that the pursuit would entail. I existed completely in the awareness alone, in that galvanized state of new perceptivity, and then, without meditation, I knew that for the first time since some lost point in my youth, everything had come into focus again. I thought that I knew why I lived.

I have felt it necessary to define the force of this emotion because this emotion was to bring me again, for a short time, into an active role in this strange relationship, and the justification of my actions must lie in part in the rightness, the inevitability of my feeling on this first night as we listened to antique music which, by its very incongruity, had plunged me into this experience of the immediate, of myself as collected, like an athlete ready to spring forward at a starting line, on the very pitch and point of the present. The rest of the evening was, of course, an anticlimax. During the remainder of the music I found myself in several unguarded moments staring at Milly's face with eyes which, had they been observed, would surely have been described as greedy, for I felt my greed. But when the music was over and conversation between the four of us picked up again, I was ready to leave. It was late. We were once more on the subject of my work. I had no interest in discussing it, I wanted to save that, and the whole world of value that it carried, for Milly. Let her take *that* from me, when we found our time, as she had taken these other qualities from them in time past.

But still, out of their rarefied world, they questioned me—Dan ingenuously, Milly quite seriously, Freddie with his air of sly knowledge beyond ours. I said what could be said, so late on a liquor-soaked evening, about the function of liberal journalism, until at last Freddie made the expected remark about starry-eyed unrealities. I almost loved him for it. It was so right that he should have said it. It brought the discussion to an end, and it gave me a point at which to begin.

I asked him where he lived, and when he told me, I suggested that we walk together down a stretch of Madison Avenue to clear our heads. He seemed glad to. When we left, Milly laid her hands on my arm for a moment in a way that made me tremble, and I did not very much want to look at Dan.

I have had my uncertainties. I have had moments, yes, hours, when I have heard myself saying, *I want assurance, I want someone to tell me that I am doing the thing that is right*. Down twenty wintry blocks Freddie walked with me, and I had no such uncertainties then, no, not then, nor over that nightcap at last in an empty bar when, as before, I plied him with questions, trying to trap him. I could not know what it was that I wanted him to say, but I knew that there was something he could say. He seemed a villain. And, *Say, say, say*, every question of mine beguiled him, but he would say nothing, he was all clever, befuddled friendliness.

"Come often," he had said to me at dinner—but who was *he*, to say that?

2

Not greed; no, after that first discovery of what could yet be, not greediness. Call it hunger. Hunger has a strange capacity of emulating the thing that it is not: when you feel hunger, the sensation is of something that is eating *you*, gnawing at the empty bowels, at the stomach groaning as it shrinks. Something like this is what that desire became, so painfully engrossing that I was able to tell myself that I had never loved before. But to feed that hunger was another matter from feeling it. The feeling of it had come like an assault, a sudden blow, had struck me down in empty aches, a visceral agony of longings. The feeding required, quite simply, a plan, a strategy, and that I did not yet have. But I thought that I knew now why I lived.

I went constantly to that great, dark apartment on upper Fifth Avenue. I went at the hours that I could manage, but what I could not manage was to be alone with Milly. Before dinner, at dinner, after dinner, it was always the same: Dan was there, and usually Freddie, too. Twice I telephoned and asked her to meet me for lunch, and each time she brought both of them along: she had just stopped by at the gallery on her way to meet me. Two or three times I tried to arrange that we have a drink together after I could leave my office: once she brought Freddie, and the other times she could not, she said, manage a meeting.

She was all charm and loveliness. Always there were those embraces, the sweet smelling arms in my arms, on my shoulders, the glad and, to me, meaningless kiss of welcome, and, when I tried to make it different, the just perceptible stiffening in her body that yet was not allowed to disrupt her willed ease. But clearly she knew now why I came! Through the foolish blur of sentimental benignity into which the four of us would sink, I would sit silently and let my eyes settle heavily on her face, while her eyes sought a flurried escape, and Freddie's burned suspiciously on me, and Dan's, impervious to all this interchange, turned inward upon his scorched self. I could not press hard: I knew that to have her at all, I had to accept the group benignity. If I disrupted that now, then all was lost. And so, under the surface, this was our skirmish: she to keep me without having me; I to keep the circle intact until I could have her.

Under that surface flowed other currents that were deep and strange and that I could not chart, and did not much want to. But it was impossible not to feel at all times the difference in the two men, and the split in Milly that their difference seemed to compel. For Dan, Freddie felt and exercised a nervous and aggressive protection, but of this, as almost of Freddie himself, Dan was unaware, or seemed to be. Freddie was simply a fact, he was simply *there*, useful, perhaps indispensable, but in no need, apparently, of Dan's particular regard. Milly's he had, and in Milly's life and nerves his nerves played a part; they altered her, changed her constantly from Dan's warm, sisterly companion to Freddie's own alert, rather cold, sharp, spasmodic, suspicious—well, *what?*

That is what I could not fathom: *what?* And yet, this split that always ran through her and through her conduct on every occasion, made me suffer, made me burn with impatience, and burn with desire for the woman who was not yet there at all and whom I could create and save from both the sentimentality and the threat of fury in the two false women that she was.

And in doing so, I might, besides, save myself from my own odd kind of loneliness and misery. For I had these. But how? *How?*

I went there one afternoon early in March at three o'clock, left my desk two hours early, and found her alone at last. She was startled, and covered her alarm with chatter. There was no embrace that day, no quick kiss; but a swift retreat into a flutter of "Darling, how nice, come in, I'll get . . . I have. . . . Tea, darling? But it's so early . . . I'll ring."

I followed her across the room and caught her arm. "No, don't, Milly. I don't want tea." And I laughed with a silly feeling of triumph. "It is early, isn't it?"

She backed away from me into the center of that huge, high room, and standing there in a plain black dress, she looked small and lonely. My heart stirred for her.

"What is it, Grant?" she asked with a kind of meek quietness. "Is anything wrong?"

"No, not really, I think," I said.

"But possibly?"

"Well, just possibly." I took a few steps toward her.

"What is it?"

I stopped, charged with a sense of our being alone together, and standing so near her now, with the possibility of everything that I thought I wanted so near, I lost my resolution for a moment. I had in my plan two simple steps. I hoped that I would not have to take the second, which might mean losing her entirely, but I had been determined to, if she made it necessary. Now, gone all soft in my stomach and my legs with a mingling of fear and desire, I could hardly bring myself to take the first.

She moved suddenly. The heavy draperies at the long windows stood open, and a bleak gray light crept, as it were, into the room, where only a heavily shaded lamp or two brightened the late winter gloom. Milly crossed her arms over her breasts, as though this light were cold, and then walked to a window and stood looking out. I followed her and, standing behind her, looked out, too. The Park was desolate from that high view: trees bare of leaves still, rocks jutting cruelly out of soiled fringes of half-melted snow, water still leaden-colored and half-frozen.

"In another month . . ." she began.

That helped me. "Let it be our month," I said impulsively, and without allowing her to turn to me, I put my arms around her and my face in her hair, and simply held her as gently as I could. She did not stir, but stood stiffly in my arms as if waiting.

I lowered my head until my mouth was on her cheek. Then she turned in my arms and, her hands pressed against my shoulders and her head bent down, lips twisted and brows intently furrowed, she pushed away from me. My arms tightened. It was her quietness that surprised me, alarmed me and made me hope, too, as for a moment we struggled against each other. Then her resistance stopped, and she fell against my chest. I held her gently again.

"Darling, I'm not going to lose you again. I did once—a stupid brute of a kid. This is different. This is all that matters to me now."

She would not look at me. She said, "This is impossible," and strained away from me again.

I held her firmly, pulling her close, forced her face up, saw how her eyes were clenched shut, her lips pressed tightly together, and yet I kissed her. It was no kiss, that meeting of my mouth and her cold, hard mouth—no kiss at all, and it shamed me. I let her go abruptly. She stood still for a moment, and when she looked at me, her face was white and shaken, and she was not angry, but dismayed. "You see? Nothing. Impossible!" and perhaps because her voice trembled, she shook her head impatiently. I saw how small strands of that closely combed blond hair had detached themselves and stood apart.

I turned away from her and from the window, and looked into the gloomy room. "Do you dislike me?"

"Grant!"

"Are you afraid?"

"Not that either."

"Well?"

"It's just impossible—"

"If you would permit yourself—"

"One doesn't, in such a thing, permit or not permit! Good God, Grant—"

"I tell you," I cried out, almost wheeling, "I won't lose you! Not again. I won't let you—not."

She bowed her head, put her hands together at her waist, and laughed briefly, without either mirth or malice.

"Why are you laughing?"

"This is bitter," she said, and looked up at me for the first time with a plea, as if I could help her, or would help the situation. I stared back at her in the only way I could, in a kind of sullenness of desire, and we stood for a long time in a static transfixion, as the gray light gathered darkness.

Then she sighed sharply and began to walk about the room, pulling at the chains of lamps, pushing at switches. Dim details of carved wood, embroidery, gilt frames, and painted canvas leapt out of the gloom into full objects, until we stood in light. She found a leather box of cigarettes and came to me, holding it open, and when I only stared at her, she walked on. She settled down in the corner of a large sofa, her knees drawn up under her, and said, "Come and sit down."

I felt heavy and inert, and it required a kind of effort to walk to the place where she sat. Heavily, I sat beside her, and she leaned toward me and put eager hands on my forearm. Now her face was positively alight with happiness, glowing with it, as her hair glowed golden under the lamplight, as her moist, parted lips gleamed in it. Maddening! And she said, "I can't lose you either, darling. I couldn't bear it. Really. And why should we lose each other, even talk of it? Hasn't it been a pleasure, these past two months, being together in the way that we first were?"

"It's not enough," I said.

"It's everything. It's what we *can* have!"

"Not enough for me," I said. "It's only painful."

"It's what we can have. It's everything. It's friendship. It's what we've always had."

"Always?"

"Should always have had."

I hesitated. Then I said, "It's perverse."

Her hands drew sharply away from my arm, where her fingers had tightened. Her face grew sad slowly, almost as if light faded in it, and when she spoke, it was no longer with enthusiasm, but very quietly. "No," she said. "What you want —that, for us, would be perverse."

After a moment, I asked, "Aren't you a woman?"

Almost easily she returned her answer. "I think so, Grant."

"But are you? If you are—"

"Haven't I made a woman's choice?"

"Have you?"

"Certainly!" That she said sharply, with an edge of anger.

"I wonder."

She stood up. "Why can't you allow it? As you would for another woman who is committed?"

I stood up, too, and seized her arms. "Because I love you until I'm half sick, and I don't think it would have happened to me if for a moment I felt that you already had love, or knew what it is. Committed! Why can't you say *married?*"

"Ah!" she said on a long, despairing breath, and looking down on my hands where they gripped her arms, she said, "You're hurting me."

I let her go.

"You're arrogant," she said quietly.

"No, no." I threw out my hands. "It's not that at all. Please don't say that, or think it. Listen, before you, in this, really, I'm—I'm just crawling."

"Don't do that either. Can't you just be easy? Can't you just come here, as you have, and be with us? It's been wonderful. More than I could have asked for. Because I thought we *had* lost you. Forever. And our meeting again, it's been, well, just pure *bounty*. Isn't that all we can ask? And can't it be enough? Can't you just be—well, *equal?*"

Equal! It shook alive some echo of anger down sealed corridors of mind, and I said quickly, "No. It's too painful, and too pointless. I'll have to get out."

"What does that mean?"

"Mean? Get out? It means leave you with Dan and Freddie." I turned and started across the room to the carved doors.

"Grant!" she called after me. I hesitated and looked back at her. Across the room, I could see her face shining with tears. Once again she looked small and forlorn, really pitiable.

"Yes?"

"You'll come back soon, won't you, Grant?"

It was the moment of the second step. I took it. "You know when, Milly," I said evenly, and I turned, and kept on going, out, and down.

For a week nothing at all happened and I began to see myself as I imagined that she was seeing me: arrogant, indeed, and less and worse—an impertinent ass who felt that he could walk into any life and order it to his will, who did not hesitate after an absence of a decade to thrust himself into a situation and declare that this must be altered, and that, and in these considerably drastic ways. And yet, that picture was entirely false to my feelings. It was not, I assured myself, the picture that her own responses had communicated to me on that afternoon when we were alone together. Certainly it was not my picture of myself. Obsessed as I was with need of her (and this need became almost intolerable as the days passed, and I did not see her), groveling under the weight of yearning to have her truly present in my life, I was equally certain that her life demanded me, or at least some other man than either friend Freddie or her husband Dan, in hers. This was the extent of my egotism: not arrogance, I assured myself, not even only desire, but the whole thing, love, which wishes equally to give and to take, and knows no difference between them, does both at once, is both, is one.

And is everything, usurps everything. Fulfilled, it makes everything else go, gives everything else its motive, its point and meaning; unfulfilled, corrupts everything, eats like an acid through the most closely woven cloth of habit and of work. So I said to myself, not only in order to stave off the uncomfortable alternative which might in fact be Milly's view of me, but also in order to hold on to at least some remnants of effectiveness and order in my job, on which I also depended. It was not easy to persist in this persuasion, and before a week had passed, I was almost ready to go back to Milly uninvited on her terms. Then one day Dan telephoned.

He said that he was calling for Milly, who wanted me to come for dinner two evenings later and to a Landowska concert afterward. I said, after a struggle, that I was working on a special assignment that demanded my evenings. He said that he was sorry and that I shouldn't stay away much longer. I told him that just then I could not help it, and put down the telephone with the fugal strains of Scarlatti in my ears, and a bitter memory of her loveliness on that first night that I had seen her again, after the long lapse of years.

In three more days Milly telephoned. She hoped that I could meet them all for lunch next day.

"I can't," I told her, as angry as I was relieved.

"We've missed you."

"I've more than missed you."

"Are you very busy?"

"No, and one always has lunch somewhere."

There was a silence. I waited. Not even her breath came over the wire, and at last I said, "Milly?"

"Yes?"

"Oh, I thought you'd gone."

Another pause, and then she said, "Will you have lunch with me?"

"Of course."

The rest was hurried and brief. The St. Regis. At one o'clock. Good-by. And next day we met among the white columns and the mahogany and the bright green palms. Milly, in a dark blue suit, with a small hat that seemed to be all veiling, and small brown furs at her neck, was waiting for me in a high, thronelike chair from which she waved when I entered, and then came toward me through the little crowd of lingering people. "Hello, darling. How nice!" She took my arm and pressed it with gentle intimacy.

"Thank you for coming," I said, and tried to say it in such a way that she would know that I meant much more than I said. To the innuendo of my tone she was impervious, smiling brightly, clinging to my arm, and saying only, "Darling, you look tired, you've been working too hard."

We were going down steps toward the dining room. I said, "No. I haven't been working at all, I'm afraid."

"But you told Dan—"

"You believed that?"

She hesitated. "It was a lovely concert. I'm sorry you didn't come."

"You couldn't have expected me to."

She hesitated again before she said, "Let's have a pleasant lunch, Grant, darling."

"Darling!" I burst out.

"Yes?"

"That word! And pleasant, unpleasant, lovely, unlovely! Good God, isn't this the point when our words are going to begin to mean something? Or why did you come?" I said it all as bitterly as I could, as I felt it. Milly glanced at me with only a little surprise before the expectant look in her face dimmed out and she sagged perceptibly on my arm. She said nothing.

"For two, sir?"

"Please."

It was luncheon of a sort with which I was no longer familiar. We sat side by side on an upholstered banquette and sipped, at Milly's suggestion, a sherry most delicately dry. The refined circumstances and Milly's exquisite presence gave me the feeling once more of being outside, a stranger, and as my only possible approach to her, I clung to the blunt, hard tone that I had taken in the corridor outside the dining room.

"This sherry—what's it called?"

She smiled and told me the name.

"This room, those people out there, you—have you any idea how expensive you look?"

"Not only, I hope, expensive."

"No, damn it, of course not. I wish that it were only expensive."

"I don't understand you."

"Oh yes, you do. You're so beautiful that I can't look at

you without pain, but I have to look over an impossible distance." There was less than a foot between us, and I could see her hands tremble.

Without turning to me, she said, "You make that distance. I don't feel it. For me, it's as it always has been. I feel very close to you. If you don't, it's your doing."

"No. It's the doing of a couple of different worlds."

"Worlds?"

"I have some idea of the one you live in, but I don't think you have the remotest idea of mine."

"We've tried to get you to talk about your work, Grant."

I did not know how far to trust her naïveté, and only said, "We!"

"Yes. We're all fascinated, but it's you who hold back."

I laughed briefly, watched a waiter's hands set down silver serving dishes before us and lift covers, and when they had finished, I said, "The difference is not one that talk will bridge. And it's between you and me only."

She looked at me with eyes suddenly troubled. "But Grant, you don't mean, do you—?"

"What?"

"You do want our friendship, don't you? *Our* friendship—Dan's, and Freddie's, too?"

"Yes, yes, of course. That, too. But first, if there's to be anything at all, there is us, alone."

She looked down at her plate and shoved at a piece of parsley with her fork. Then she took some food. I ate, too. We sat in silence. At last she put down her fork and looked at me. "And afterward?" she asked.

"Afterward?"

"After we've had—this."

"This?" I pressed.

"This that you want."

I covered her hand on the table's edge with mine. "I see no afterward," I told her.

"But there must be. And what will it be like? You might say you see no future. Such a thing can't have a future, can it? We'll never, in lamplight, descant upon the themes of art and song. Or anything. No future. But an afterward—yes. And what will it be? That's what I have to know."

In that agitated speech, she made the only literary allusion I was ever to hear from her, and it gave me courage. If now she could express her dilemma through a lyric, she was not, I thought, as agitated as she seemed. I said, "How can you know? I love you. That's what I know. Twenty-four hours a day. And I can't just live around you in an aimless daze."

"I love you, too," she said.

"But you can't trust me."

"Trust you to what?"

"To make you happy." I pressed her hand tightly, and she looked at me.

"How can I know?" she asked. "I love them, too. Dan and Freddie. I love all of you."

"All in the same way? You love Dan as you love Freddie?"

"No, of course not."

"Or me, as you love Dan?"

"No."

And then my real question: "Or Freddie, as you do me?"

She hesitated and at last said, "Well—no."

"Well, then," I said quickly, "have us all, but have each of us in the way that you can."

"But three? And one of them you?"

"Surely you don't expect me to be Freddie!"

"I'm afraid."

"I asked you that. You said that you were not afraid. But I know that you are. And in a deeper way than you know. But you needn't be, if you'll let me—if you'll admit me as a man, in my own right, and once find the courage to be your whole self, a woman."

She answered humbly. "I want you with us, I don't want to lose you."

I lifted her taut hand and kissed her wrist, and the hand grew limp.

"The waiter," she said, lowering her arm. I clung to her hand on the seat between us. "I'd like coffee, please," she said. "And a brandy." And then presently, detaching her hand from mine, "Different worlds. How are they different? What *is* my world?"

"Isn't it like this?" I asked, turning the brandy snifter before me in my hands. "Not quite a bell jar, but nearly? Lovely and shining and self-contained, made to concentrate essences, and through this small opening admitting very little from outside?"

"We have, of course, our obligation to Dan," she said.

"Ah, yes," I answered. "That. But I only want to persuade you that you have another to yourself, as I have to myself."

"And your world, Grant? How is it so different?"

"It involves people, many people, not just a few who can buy pictures, many people, and the way people live together, what people need to live at all."

"It's more humane than mine, you're saying?"

"Just more human, because it includes more. It's a public world; yours is private. Being public, mine values ideas; yours values things. Yours is a world of sensation and nuance; mine of fairly rough struggle, passions. Forgive my pomposity."

"You make it all sound very clear cut," she said, looking down in her bag, hunting through it. "Shall we go?" And without saying more, she rose, dropped a bill on the salver with the check, and stepped down from the raised banquette. "This

lunch is the pleasure of the closed, expensive world," she murmured, scarcely looking at me, and went out, ahead. I followed
her, and it was only when we came into Fifty-fifth Street and
she turned to me under the marquee that I saw she was crying.

My heart shrank: literary allusion or not, she was forcing
herself to say good-by; I had lost. And I felt an impulsive rush
of cruelty. "Surely nothing that I said can be worth your tears."

Her face was soft and wounded. She brushed at her eyes
with her handkerchief, and she said, "Yes, enough of what you
said is true or true enough to make me—" She broke off impatiently and blew her lovely nose.

"Make you what?"

"I've never seen your apartment, Grant. Take me there,
won't you?"

In my abrupt humiliation, I gasped and used her word,
"Darling!"

I took her arm and we turned into Fifth Avenue and walked
silently for a while in the melting, late March afternoon, on
slushy sidewalks. She walked with her head down and passively
allowed me to steer her through the crowds. There was a
rather terrible sense of joyless fatality about that walk, about
her, even about the delicate arch of her bent neck over the
brown furs, under the frivolous hat. We got on a bus presently
and as we rode downtown in silence, it occurred to me, as,
day after day, it had to every man of good will, that we were
in the infamous month of *Anschluss,* when an unwilling Austria
submitted to a tyranny that she was half-convinced was necessary to survival. Now the thought of a decreed debasement
impelled me to turn sharply to Milly, to try to find some warm
thing to say to her. She looked at me and smiled gently, almost
shyly, and her smile made it unnecessary to say anything. I let
my shoulder rest against hers and pressed her arm, which I still
held.

At Tenth Street, we got off the bus and walked the few blocks east to my building, and then I led her up the three flights of stairs to the shabby two-room affair that was my apartment. As soon as we entered, she stopped before the false fireplace, and stared up at the poster from Barcelona that I had tacked up over the Travertine marble mantel. It was a large sheet, perhaps five feet by five, and it showed in the lower foreground a phalanx of bare, lifted arms, and above them, printed on a blue sky in letters of blood, the single word *Salud.*

"*Salud,*" I rather foolishly said to Milly, who turned and came surprisingly into my arms. Our lips just touched, and there was a mingling of breath, and I said to myself, *easy, easy,* as our lips trembled over that promise of a kiss. Then Milly lifted her hands to remove her hat, and I released her. She dropped the hat on a chair, unfastened the furs at her neck and let them fall beside it, and then unbuttoned her jacket and tossed that on the chair, too. She was wearing a filmy white blouse that gave her a rather prim air. Then she sat down on a worn studio couch and peered at an anti-fascist calendar drawing by Gropper that hung on the wall beside her.

"So this is where you live. It is different. You're right, I see—"

I sat beside her and pulled her softly back into my arms. "Dearest girl, we have a language," I said, and then began that first kiss, which must do everything for me and undo so much of tightness and of fear in her. Gently, gently it began, that first soft trembling of the lips together again, and then more firmly pressing, then parting, the hot breath together, the tongue slowly pressing, exploring, finding, mouths opening together, pushing, searching, sucking, deep, deep, bodies straining together, straining, arching, and then, "Oh," she moaned suddenly and long, and collapsed against me, her head down on my chest. I murmured in her hair and stroked her, her back, her shoulders, her neck, her cheek, then lowered her body in my arms, and then began again, first softly, softly, lips quivering, resistance flowing away again, lips opening, tongue, breath, pressing, begging, demanding, deep, deep, and longer now, longer, bodies straining again, forcing, arms tight around, tight, tight, and then again "Oh-h," the sudden moan, the quick collapse, and something torn away, something broken.

"Darling, darling," murmured only, and then my arms under her, lifting her. I carried her into the bedroom, where the light was gray, and laid her on my bed, helped her with her clothes, then pulled off my own. When I came to her, I put my face on her stomach, touched her small, girllike breasts, brushed tenderly the maidenly flaxen hair, then stretched beside her, flesh against flesh now, soft and hard, hot, and the kiss again, slow, slow, more softly, more softly, the draining away of will and separateness, then harder, deeper, harder, deeper, longer, longer, wash, wash, wash, and now no separateness, entirely together, no will, no nothing but slow wash and wash of hot blood and then slow rock, rock of ocean in us, wash and rock, wash and rock, wash and rock, and oh! she was mine, she *was* mine.

And so, in a sense, April of that year became our month.

3

April, May, and half of June. It was lovely, and it was strange, too, because it was, alas, incomplete, as perhaps I should have known that it would be, since it is almost certainly true that any idyl must also be a fragment. Yet one may ask whether any life, in all its parts, can be one and whole, and find, perhaps, in the very nature of things, some justification for the partialities of our experience.

That it was an idyl, even under the somewhat grimy circumstances of my life, is true. At the end of March I gave up my downtown apartment and took a single room at monthly rates in a midtown hotel, just a step across the street from my office, and here Milly came, when we both could manage, during my lunch hour. Sometimes she brought my lunch for me; sometimes we had sandwiches sent up for us. That was our place and our time, above the crash and bang of Forty-sixth Street traffic, in an impersonal box of a room where soot was always on the sills, with metal furniture finished in a brown, halfhearted simulation of wood, with a hard, worn carpet on the floor and two pink and blue and pale green prints of romantic subjects in gilt frames on the dun walls. The only merit of this place was its convenience and the fact that, just because it was so rather horribly neutral, we could, when we were together, be impervious to it.

That was our poor fragment of an idyl, closed off from nearly everything, and confined almost entirely to that room, that hour. Twice Milly appeared, after a hurried pay-phone call, rather late at night, on some ruse, in a pitiable attempt to show that, on our account, she was willing to take that risk. But more she would not risk. I tried to persuade her to come away for just one week end, to say that she had to go up to Albany and then go, instead, to Fire Island or some country hotel, so that we could have at least two days together, uninterrupted, in the spring. But she would not. She would not, as she would not let our relationship touch the rest of her life. And so, in the end, it became almost intolerable—in minor ways for me, in a major way for her.

She changed for me. She changed, as I had hoped for her sake that she could: but the terrible thing was that she changed for me alone and not in her whole person, so that for her this was merely a further act of self-division. We would meet in that implausible room and she was entirely mine and entirely what I would have had her be: frank in her passion and wanton with it, and afterward, in the murmuring relaxed tenderness that proved the consummation, gentle and humorous, alert and interested if we talked (and these occasions were our only time for talk), sometimes sleepy. Sometimes she said, "I want to sleep here for a while," and I would leave her in that bed. When I came back at the end of the afternoon, the room was entirely in order again, as though no one had been there at all, but mingling with the dry, city air of the room, a faint ghost of her perfume. Or we would lie in that rumpled bed and talk—I would talk, I suppose—talk in those months of Spain and Germany and Roosevelt. I tried to interest her in the world of ideas and events within which my work existed, and she would listen with a sweet patience, but she had, in fact, no real interest in ideas or events, and listened only on my account, her body close, her mind either empty or away, and words would drag and stall at last, and we would dress again, and part in the street presently, with a last quick gesture of embrace. And then if in the evening I went to the apartment on Fifth Avenue, as I often did, it was almost as if we had not had that gulp of passion at all, only a few hours before, almost as if we had nothing between us that was our own. A quick pressure of the hand, a word of endearment delivered *sotto voce* to set it off from all the loose endearments she was given to, a wry smile, a long glance: these were the conventionally secret and unsatisfactory tokens of our conspiracy, the intolerable reminders that our love had no relation to anything outside and that, because it had none, was hardly even a deceit. And while it is true enough that I had had no very clear expectations of what should come of it, I had certainly miscalculated the human chemistry, which I had thought to have certain inevitable characteristics. On the contrary. Those categories of an outmoded psychology—head, heart, and loins—seemed not at all outmoded here, for Milly's head, if one means the calculating portion, was Freddie's still (there *was* some alliance there that I could not fathom, and an alliance unaltered by my intrusion or the fact of *our* alliance); and her heart, if one means the merely sympathetic nature, was Dan's, as before; and the third was mine. And this surely was an intolerable situation for her.

My hope had been that she would heal her divisions and find an identity through me. Hers seemed to be to find it *in* us, in all of us—to divide and extend herself, and by binding us together in the constantly revived and reconsidered *ambiente* of the shared experience of our youth, somehow bind her life together, and her being. It is impossible to say to what extent *being* is autonomous, and to what extent it exists in relationship, or even in what intricate way these two are balanced in the human economy, but here there was no balance at all, there was only a kind of war. And as I lived with her and with them in this queer warfare, it seemed to me, as it had on my first evening with them, that it was Freddie who, somehow, was at the root of it, Freddie who held the secret and Freddie who did the first damage, Freddie who most needed them, and Freddie, therefore, who most injured her. That was the line I must pursue if our love was to be of any use at all, or even if it was to survive.

In those three months, on the occasions when the four of us were together, it was always Freddie that I had been watching, but I learned nothing. We were frequently together, chiefly at concerts but occasionally at the theater, and one week end we spent in the country, and then we walked and swam together as in the old days. Freddie and Dan and I were all off our swimming form and short of wind, but Milly was as good as ever, and when she dived, she was a marvel. Watching her in perfect control of that body that was so meaninglessly mine, I felt a stab of jealousy that almost tempted me to take Freddie aside and blurt out the truth to him, tell him and shatter him, once and for all. But then, watching him in his gawking approval of Milly's grace as, over and over, she went off that high board like a bird, I relaxed again: he seemed too stupidly happy to disturb, too innocently admiring, suddenly, to merit suspicion of anything. I would have to find another time, some other means.

An interruption loomed ahead. As May of that year came toward an end, and war in Europe became a clear inevitability, this country seemed to enter upon a period of industrial prosperity, and the newspapers wrote of what they called the "Recovery." My editor, who viewed the boom with a properly ironic suspicion, asked me to undertake a swing through the major industrial areas in the country and to write a series of on-the-spot reports for the magazine. The project would take most of the summer. Dan and Milly, meanwhile, had taken a place for the summer on the Connecticut shore, where they had previously been, and while this had not been said, Freddie, I suspected, would spend most of his summer with them, or at least as much of it as was left free to him by the business of the gallery, which they closed during July and August.

"If you could come with me—that would make it mean something!"

We were on my bed, I half sitting up, she lying, her shoulders on my arm where I leaned upon my elbow. That evening I was to leave for Detroit.

"Ah, Grant—don't plague us with impossibles."

"I know."

She looked up into my face. "You're not satisfied?"

I could not answer. Instead, I asked what I already knew. "You never go to Silverton in the summers any more?"

"The Ford house is up for sale. We've told you, haven't we?"

"Why is that?"

"It would be impossible for Dan. All his deepest memories are there, the reminders would be constant."

"But he has his father's business, you live in his father's apartment—"

"I think that we should move. To some wholly new place. Dan's not getting better. Have you noticed? He broods more and more."

I hesitated to say what I had long wanted to say. "Don't you think you miscalculate Dan's needs?"

"How?"

"Protecting him as you do, you imprison him in a way. Imprison him with nothing, or with nothing but the very thing you want him to overcome. But he has no means of overcoming it."

She looked at me gravely. "I hope you're not right," she said.

"Doesn't Dan ever want to go back there, to Silverton?"

"He never speaks of it."

"Freddie—well, of course, he positively doesn't want to, does he?"

"No, I don't think he does."

"Did you ever meet his parents?"

"Freddie's?"

"Yes."

"No, I never did. They really mean nothing to him."

"That's curious though, don't you think, Milly?"

"Is it?"

"No connection at all, I mean. Just a blank. After the youthful revolt, most people make an adjustment—they want *some* connection—"

"Hasn't it occurred to you that more is curious in our situation than only Freddie? Hasn't it occurred to you that here we are, four of us, and none of us really has parents? You and Dan have none in fact. And in effect, Freddie and I have none. That's perhaps what links us."

Her remarks made me impatient, and "Orphans in the storm!" I sneered mildly.

"Well, yes, if you wish."

"Sweetheart, don't be silly. You're nothing like Freddie. Your mother is also really dead. And your father—he never had any room left for you, did he? But Freddie—he's just a snob, don't you see?"

"No, no."

"What is Freddie anyway? What's he like inside? Sometimes I have no sense of him at all, as a person."

"What a strange remark from you, Grant, having known him ever since you were a boy."

"I know. But sometimes I don't really know him at all. I mean—I feel there is a kind of emptiness in him that is not to be known, because there's nothing."

"Oh, you're being unfair!"

"And at other times I feel strongly that what is there is some secret, something concealed and sinister—"

"Nonsense."

"And I can't relate him now, very much, to the boy he was. In those slick, shoulder-padded gabardines he wears, with his sucking attachment to you and Dan—it's just hard to believe—that kid in overalls who could kill a crow with a slingshot!"

"Well. . . ."

"Freddie's really a fascist, I think."

"Oh, nonsense!"

"Not only politically. Although there, too, I'll venture. But in a larger sense than in his rationalized attitudes alone, as towards Spain, for example. Temperamentally, I mean. The emotional ruthlessness. The absence of inner support that impels him to his external aggressiveness—in his personal relationships, I mean. Notably, of course, with you and Dan."

"Now you're being silly!" she laughed.

"Silly? I wonder. Dan and Freddie together—Dan's like a small, highly cultivated, peace-loving country that's just been moved in on."

"Ridiculous. Freddie is just marvelous for Dan, he's been a lifesaver in the gallery, for example. And as for other ways—"

"How necessary is he to the gallery, really?"

"Well, *you* know, Grant—or don't you?"

"I know he does a lot there. I know he thinks he's necessary. And that Dan does, too. But in a real sense, *is* he?"

"Of course. It's really Freddie who's responsible for the present character of the gallery, for all the changes. Dan's father was mainly interested in eighteenth-century French and British pictures. Now it's contemporary and modern, bright, even Americans—"

"But wouldn't it be better for Dan if Dan were allowed to

have the full responsibility now? Perhaps that was impossible at first. But now. Wouldn't it be?"

"I can't imagine it."

"I can," I said. "It's what Dan needs."

She closed her eyes and stirred restlessly on my arm, then lifted her hand and put it on my chest. "Stop talking, dear. Our time is passing."

"Ah, Milly—" I slid down beside her. "How stubborn you are, under this soft outside!" Her arm went round my neck, her mouth brushed slowly over mine, back and forth, our arms tightened, and we were in the embrace. How different now, how quickly, with the habit of our life, the separateness flowed away and she was there for me! Then slowly, slowly. . . .

"I'll miss you so," she murmured. "I'll miss you so."

"I'll miss you," I murmured in reply. "I'll miss you."

"Oh, Grant, dear Grant—"

"You do love me?"

Slowly, slowly, our mouths lying lightly together, breath mingling. "Grant, Grant," she said, her arms tightening.

"You love me most?"

Her mouth on mine, clamped, but no words in reply, as faster now, faster, and I lifted my head.

"You love me most?"

"Grant, dearest, dearest."

"You love me most. Say it. Say it. Oh, say it!"

Her eyes were shut. "Dearest, dearest. . . ."

"And get rid of Freddie."

Her body jerked, her arms tightened, "I'm not listening!" she cried, and the shuddering spasm was upon us. Then, in the morbid quiet, when she opened her eyes on me again, she only repeated, "I'll miss you so," as if no outrage had been committed, and I did not then press my point.

We left the hotel together, and in the street she kissed me

swiftly. "Until seven, darling," she said. *Darling* was her public endearment, and her use of it now gave me pause.

They picked me up at seven, the three of them, as we had arranged. We had dinner together, and there was much of that word *darling*, then, as always when we were all together, perhaps more than always. They drove me to the airport. And when at last my plane had been called, and we stood together at the end of the runway, and the handshakes were over, and only our good-by kiss remained, I gripped her arms and my mouth touched her cheek, and I whispered, "I mean it. Get rid of Freddie! It's Freddie or me."

Too loudly she cried, "Good-by, darling, good-by," and "Good-by, good-by," the men echoed, and I went.

She would not let me do that for her.

Our communications during the summer were few, and they were for and from the group, and said nothing. I came back late in September, and when I saw them next, it was in their new apartment. Freddie had moved, too; he had moved in with them.

Do you remember? That was the month of hurricanes and Munich, and people, I said, are as much like countries as they are like weather.

4

She would not let me do that for her, but I had loved her, and I loved her still, yes, although now in a different way again (for passion, like poetry, cannot live by itself alone; it needs the bread of daily habit, the stuff of humbler actualities than itself to feed it and be transfigured by it), and I could not let her harm herself and Dan without some further effort to help her. Not yet, at least, even though now some more elaborate strategy was needed, since now she had drawn away from me again, had withdrawn more completely than ever into the Freddie-*persona*, and Freddie himself was there now, always pompously present and more officious than ever, and Dan was frailer, less steady even than before. They had all changed. Only I, it seemed, was the same.

They had changed with their surroundings. Their new apartment was high over the East River. You rose to it in an elevator that was lined with watered mirrors colored like a pool of the sea on a bright day, strange lucid green, pale and ripply, in which your reflection wavered like a monster fish as silently you rose and rose, until you emerged in their citadel of air and emptiness.

Here there were great walls of glass through which you looked out upon nothing at all but sky, or back upon the towers of Manhattan, and these, whether ghostly in evening mists or cut out in hard, isolated, daytime clarity, seemed unreal, an abstract fantasy of a city on a poster. Or these windows could be covered by pulling across them yards and yards of pleated gauze that fell from ceiling to floor in always slightly stirring folds, as if they should give forth whispers, and tinted, like the walls, in graded shades of gray. There were low, spare sofas with deep pillows and no arms, upholstered in rough materials of gray and beige and pale blue, all shot with silver, and in one wall, a low rectangular fireplace was cut, without mantel, without ornament, and there, on chromium irons, a fastidious log could blaze. Out of one wall burst a chamber (what can one call such a room that is not a room?) that was like a great shell or bell of glass, and here stood a round dining table, two tall plants with uneasy, savage leaves, and heavy tapers in ascetic standing racks. The walls of this establishment were entirely bare except for two pictures that hung with geometric precision on one wall —early Chiricos that looked out upon space as emptily as dead eyes. Every vestige of the elder Fords had been dismissed, every suggestion of their ostentatious clutter. Here was a new and terrible purity, sterility wrought into a style.

I came there as a friend, and saw at once the difference in them and in my status. Milly treated me with a gust of cool, swift verbiage that was like mockery, it was at once so intimate and so disengaged. There was no way of meeting her, or of laying the groundwork for what was to come next, either, except by boldness, and as soon as we were alone, I said, "Now you dislike me."

"Darling!" she cried. "Don't be absurd!"

"I think I've hurt you."

"*How?*" High incredulousness.

"That business about Freddie."

"Freddie? But darling, Freddie's no problem!"

I spoke softly, dejectedly. "You understand, I hope, that I'm fond of Freddie. I like him fine, it's only—"

"But of course! Of course!"

"Please, Milly—"

"But who would suggest that you don't?"

"No one, I hope. But what I want to say is—the reason that —I would never have—I said that—"

She laughed. "Why are you making things so difficult for yourself, darling? No one's accusing you of anything."

"I want to be plain. I want this all to be straight. I did drive you away from me, and by one remark. My reason was: I do honestly think that Freddie's bad for Dan. Also for you."

Her chin sharpened a little but she never ceased to smile. "Darling, Grant, I seem to remember that you were worried only about losing me."

"Yes."

"And you haven't lost me, have you?"

"Haven't I?"

"Dear Grant, why would you be here?"

"All right," I said.

"And I haven't lost you, have I?"

"No."

"Well, then— Everything's lovely."

"But Freddie—"

"Freddie! Freddie! *He's* not lost to us."

"No, certainly not."

"Well—?"

She was as impossible as that. And how I had miscalculated! Some consolidation of temperament had taken place: gone, really, were both the cold agitation of speech that I had associated with Freddie, and the friendly composure that seemed to have belonged to Dan; or rather, part of each had gone and the two had come together in a cold composure; but what was wholly gone was the deeper, warmer grace that briefly had been mine. More simply, one can describe the change in action: some net had been drawn closer. Into it she had pulled those of whom she could be sure. She could not be sure of me, and I was now outside it, perhaps I was even viewed as dangerous. I think that already she wished that I would leave them, but nothing had reached the necessary stage of clarity at which she could say so plainly, and thus I was to be tolerated while we executed, for how long I could not know, this fantastic verbal dance in which all realities were denied.

But presently another opportunity presented itself, and I began again. "Consider Freddie then," I said. "Think of it from his point of view."

"Of what, Grant?"

"Of the situation *he's* in."

"You mean his living here? It's a convenience for all of us, an obvious convenience."

"Not that, particularly, but that too. It rather denies him the possibility of a private life, doesn't it, if he has any such inclination? But really I mean the constant secondary role that he plays in every way."

"Secondary role," she reflected. "In *which* ways?"

"Is it good for a man to have no life of his own, not even a professional life, to be so completely identified with the interests of *others?*"

"Grant, Freddie's a free man. He can choose anything for himself that he wants."

"Yes!"

"But, of course, he can."

"He'll need some help, I'm afraid, at this stage."

"Help?"

"Help."

"From you, Grant?"

"After a period in which the morale has been sapped—"

She stopped me, and for the first time with an impatient

speech. "Grant, it's dangerous for men to try to play God."

"Ah, yes," I said quickly. "But isn't that your wish—to be some kind of goddess?"

The sharpened chin, the fine, tightened nostrils relaxed. All hint of impatience flowed away. She stood up and smiled at me with positive benignity. "I hope that I'll always be a goddess for you, Grant," she said in the kindest voice, and laid her hand lightly on my shoulder.

I turned my head swiftly and kissed her fingers, but she drew her hand away at once and laughed. "Only a *goddess*, please! *Only* a goddess!" And she walked away from me across that large, spare room, walked silently on the thick, pale carpeting, and chuckled as she went. Yes—a warm, low, complacent, nearly self-congratulatory sound for which, ridiculous as it may seem, I can think of no other word: she chuckled.

Through these skirmishes I began to catch glimpses of a means. Indeed, in those skirmishes I was clarifying the situation for myself, and directly it was clear, I would know how I should move, what I *could* do, being outside her interests, as I now was.

Now and until the end, my motivation lay almost entirely in Dan. As Milly was more composed in a certain electric way than she had been before, Dan, as I have suggested, was less so: frailer, less steady, rather fallen in upon himself, more querulous, his happy summer face pinched and paler, his hair rapidly graying. And, with Milly, Freddie, growing rather portly, wove and wove about Dan in his curious protective dance. All that winter this went on: they wove him in, they wove me out.

One evening in December I was there in that high uncluttered place, sitting through desultory conversation, staring at the surrounding darkness in which the lights of the apartment picked out gusts of snow funneling down on low, moaning winds.

"That's bitter-looking snow," Dan said.

"Freddie, dear, draw the draperies, won't you?" Milly asked.

I thought of ragged Republican troops, ill-equipped, outnumbered, nearly routed, and when Freddie sat down again, I said, "It's colder in Spain than it is in here."

Milly glared at me and Freddie quickly said, "I went to see Picasso's 'Guernica' again today. What a pretentious mistake!"

"Borax, Freddie?" I asked, using a piece of cant that he liked to throw into his remarks on pictures.

"Of course not." He said it impatiently. "Picasso can't paint badly. But he can paint so much better."

"You don't like it, Freddie? You're practically alone in New York."

"Such political painting is, in its way, as irresponsible as his political remarks."

"What do you mean?"

"When you think of what he can do," Milly said.

"When you think of something like the 'Demoiselles d'Avignon,'" Freddie went on, "and then of this—well, this cartoon! That's what it is, of course."

"It's overrated," Dan said. "Interesting, but not very rich, is it?"

"It's rich in idea," I said.

"I mean, of course, in the painting, *as* painting."

"Is there something like that?"

"That's about all there is in painting," Freddie said. "How the painter puts on paint."

I looked up at the pictures by Chirico, and thought of his allegiances, and of the connection between them and the dead world he had always seen in his imagination, and the heavy, glistening paint seemed to me to have the sheen of death. How a painter puts on paint, I would have ventured, is finally, in the whole human mystery were we but able to observe it, as much a matter of motivation by idea, or allegiance to idea, however negative, as any other action in the world, as for example, putting down in words statements of ideas themselves. But I had no interest in pursuing this line; we had been over it before, and there was no possibility of deflecting either Dan or Freddie from their stubborn aestheticism. I had, furthermore, a wish to turn the conversation to another subject, deliberately, for a change, to test this situation; for what I had by now come to think of as the shutting in of Dan from the world outside, as the purposeful limiting and cushioning of his experience, was still a matter mostly of impression. When I asked myself for particulars, they were elusive; I had a conviction, a feeling, but I wanted evidence.

So I said as mildly as I could, "Have you seen the evening papers?" and at once felt a tightening in Milly and in Freddie. "There's a story," I went on, "that would interest you, Dan, especially—"

Milly cut in with quite inappropriate finality. "We take two morning papers, and really, with everything in the world so dreary, that's more than enough for me."

And Freddie, in his old maneuver: "Let me fill your glass, fella."

Fella! How did he really feel about me? As comradely as *that?* I was not sure. So expert had been Milly's deceit in the spring that he had never suspected what went on then between us. And what else was there to suspect? I think that it was only Milly who was made uneasy by my presence, fearful that somehow I might now let him know. A pointless fear. Dan was, of course, impervious, as essentially unaware of me as, I am convinced, he was of Freddie. We were both simply there, objects that raised no questions for him. And so perhaps Freddie did feel friendship for me, or at least as warm a friendship as his uncertainties about me allowed. Some such uncertainties he must have felt, for that I was not a partner in *his* alliance with Milly, whatever that might be, must have been perfectly clear to both of them. I said, "Thanks, Freddie, why not?" and smiled at him.

"What was it, Grant?" Dan asked.

I toyed. "What?"

"You started to say—"

"Oh, Dan," Milly cried. "*Did* Mrs. C. buy the drawings I sent her to look at?"

"Perhaps tomorrow," he said, and then to me again, "Something about a news story."

"Oh, yes," I said. "I thought perhaps you'd heard about it. It's about a theft at the Behn Studios—early this morning."

"Behn's? Really? No, I didn't hear anything about it."

"Here, Dan," Freddie said, and interposed himself between Dan and me with the inevitable pitcher. When he straightened up again, he said to Milly, "She did come in. I'm sure she'll want the drawings. She'd be a fool not to, at the price we're proposing."

Milly went on rapidly. "But Mrs. Cummings is so whimsical in her buying." In her agitation, she had named a client's name, and in their mysterious and secretive professional world, that was a laxity never permitted, even with only me to hear.

Freddie rushed ahead. "She holds out and holds out. And then is furious when she loses something that's been urged on her and that she really does want. First she must always persuade herself that the entire negotiation rests solely on *her* judgment. In the meantime, someone else may very well have acted on ours. Will you have a cocktail, Milly?"

"No more, thank you, darling," she said, and looked eagerly

toward the dining chamber, where a servant was lighting the white tapers.

Dan had, for a change, maintained his interest in a chopped-off topic, and he said, "I want to hear the rest of Grant's story. What was stolen, Grant?"

"A small Cézanne. But it wasn't that so much that was interesting, as the way the fellow tried to bring it off."

"He didn't get away with it?"

I glanced at Milly, who was studying me with a rigid eye, and I said, "Well, no, he didn't," and now I was certain that Milly knew the story I was trying to tell. The thief, it seemed, was a young art student who wanted the picture for its own sake, and he had worked out an elaborate scheme for getting it, which involved his entering the gallery by a skylight and letting himself down by a knotted rope. He had cut the picture out of its frame, rolled it, strapped it to his back, and gone back up the rope, but when he was about to escape by the skylight again, he slipped and crashed to the tiled floor of that high room, where, quite thoroughly smashed up, he lay until a night watchman found him, and died a few hours later in a hospital.

"How late we are with dinner," Milly said impatiently. "I will have another cocktail, Freddie. You'd better give us all one." And so once more the story was interrupted.

"But what happened?" Dan asked as Freddie busied himself again. I went on with the story, and when Freddie turned to Milly to pour her drink, she rose to receive it, and then spilled it.

"Damn!" she cried. "All down my dress."

Dan pulled out his handkerchief and, kneeling before her, wiped at her skirt.

"How silly of me!" she said.

"It's nothing," Dan muttered.

"So clumsy."

"Then what, Grant?" The handkerchief moved more slowly over the skirt.

"When he was about to get out of there again—"

Then Milly said it plainly. "Please, Grant!"

Dan looked quickly up at her, at Freddie, and then at me. "What is this?" he asked rather shrilly. "Some kind of plot?"

"Darling, don't be foolish. I want Grant to stop interrupting you until you're finished."

"I am finished," he said as he straightened up. "What is all this? Has it something to do with me?"

"Darling, I don't know the story. I don't know what Grant's talking about."

"What *are* you talking about, Grant?" Freddie asked ominously. He was standing, too, holding his pitcher, and his eyes, like Milly's, were not so much looking at me as trying to compel me.

I said, "There's not much more. Just as the fellow was about to escape, a night watchman came in and caught him. The police have him, and the gallery has the picture, only slightly damaged."

"Oh," said Dan, as the three of them sat down again and the tension drained slowly out of their faces. Over her glass, Milly smiled at me with a suggestion of the old warmth, as though she could count on me after all, and Freddie said, "Good! To Cézanne!" Then dinner was announced, and we went in to that round table, where there was no longer any suggestion of a head or a foot or sides, and at which we sat in all the meaningless equality of childhood, while Freddie talked quite brilliantly of Cézanne. But what preposterous thing was being done to Dan in the name of love and kindness?

Freddie's talk at dinner, following so immediately upon that demonstration of Dan's predicament, showed me in a flash not only the desperate need for action in his behalf, but the possible action itself. After dinner I said casually to Freddie, "You talk so well about pictures, and once you said you'd thought of writing about them. Why don't you?"

He looked surprised. "As a matter of fact, I have. I've been thinking recently of a book and I've been making some notes for it."

"Good. On what?"

"Something to be called *The Commerce of Culture*. Really about the history and the function of the picture dealer."

"Oh, yes. But I was thinking of criticism. Haven't you ever thought of that?"

"What's in your mind, Grant?"

"I have an idea, Freddie. Can we talk about it? Let's have lunch soon, shall we?"

"Good!" he said, pleased.

What had most impressed me earlier was that when Milly and Freddie let me give that inaccurate account of the Behn Studio theft, they were committing themselves to keeping from Dan the real story and felt quite safe in doing so. That meant that he would somehow be kept from reading about it next day; it meant that he could be closed off from even the professional gossip of Fifty-seventh Street; that he made only gestures of independence, that he was a fantastic prisoner. Without Freddie's assistance, this captivity would be impossible. And therefore, if Freddie, through an appeal to his vanity, could be pried loose from them, and Dan, thrust out of the habit of his native passivity, were forced to make those gestures real—would it not be his salvation? And Milly's, too, little as she knew in which direction her salvation lay? It all suddenly stood before me, complete and plausible, this beautiful possibility for aid. It would require, to be sure, some ruthlessness in regard to Freddie himself, but to that I was prepared to close my eyes; this was a familiar paradigm of means and ends, and my eyes were open to the greater good.

At the offices of *The New World*, I had now a certain authority and prestige. I had been there for several years, I had worked in several departments and done several kinds of writing, and, in fact, as the political situation was growing more complex, more confusing, I was doing more and more work for the back of the book, those "cultural" pages where one could write without feeling the necessity of commanding all the final answers. It was in this connection that Freddie entered, for the art columns were, of course, at the back of the magazine, and we were presently going to need a new art man. My notion was to sell Freddie to the editor for that place.

This fiasco need not be detailed in the telling. My editor was interested in Freddie's qualifications, and Freddie, perhaps for the very reason that he had never before had the opportunity of being tempted by the charming prospect of seeing his opinions in print, succumbed to my proposal with all the fascination of the amateur. He had, it seemed, some idea of becoming one of those refined collector-critics of the old school, a lesser Berenson, perhaps, but of the contemporary, and he saw in my proposal an opportunity to begin this development, a chance to bring his name, together with his prose, before a public, and the sacrifice in money that it would mean was more than balanced in his mind by the prospect of a new and brilliant kind of extension of himself. Naïve to the point of folly! It was suggested that he write a few trial reviews of current shows, and in his eagerness, he did not consider for a minute, I think, the probable consequences. I knew from the outset that a less likely staff writer on that magazine could hardly be imagined, and that it would not be very long before his peculiarly tight and class-bound views would trip him into such illiberality of judgment that he would be out. I did not have enough interest in Freddie himself to wish to do him any harm, and I might have felt some qualms about this clear interference in his affairs if I had felt that I was doing him any real harm. I was not; and I might be helping someone who had indeed been dear to me, was still, and desperately needed help. When, in January, Barcelona fell, and the tragedy of Spain was over, I felt no new fondness for Freddie, it is true—no more for Freddie than for others like him who had been either indifferent to that tragedy or frankly on the side of evil—and still, my bitterness and disappointment did not direct themselves at persons, neither at Freddie nor at all the others. It was only Dan, in this, who mattered, and the change that overtook Dan almost at once, as Freddie became engaged in these other activities, is my vindication.

It was understood, of course, that Freddie would sever his connections with The Ford Gallery if he were finally to have the place on *The New World*, but for the five or six weeks that he was writing his sample pieces, which were not for publication, he was free to maintain it. To do his pieces creditably, however—and within their limits they were very able—he necessarily had much less time to give to the gallery, and Dan, in turn, found himself in a position where he could not choose but exercise his judgment and assert his taste, his tact, his business sense. This was really the first opportunity he had had to do so with any independence, and he began to feel himself as an entity. While Milly sat somewhat stonily by, and Dan complained mildly that Freddie had abandoned him, both still expressed excited interest in his venture. And Dan positively began to change again. How thrilling is even the promise of the rebirth of a man! Milly let me feel the cold force of her dislike, but Dan's visible strengthening more than justified me as I watched Freddie in the precarious bliss of that new self-importance for which I was happy to accept the responsibility.

Milly was beyond my understanding, and necessarily; I was, as events would presently show, still ignorant of her, for all our intimacy. Thus now I could only conclude that for the sake of a wholly servile Freddie she would choose an ailing Dan. But that this was not quite the way she posed her terms of choice I had yet to learn.

My plot developed with a smoothness that should have warned me. The editor liked Freddie's preliminary pieces and asked him to come into the office and work with the staff for a few weeks before either of them made a final commitment. Freddie thus withdrew entirely from the daytime operations of The Ford Gallery. He still lived with Dan and Milly, of course; I had not yet devised means whereby he could be maneuvered out of that hold on their lives, and until I did he would continue to exercise at least an advisory control in their affairs. Yet the happy change in Dan was so great that I could hardly have in justice wished for more on his account.

On a February evening, when I came to the apartment earlier than I was expected and found Dan alone, we stood before one of the great windows and looked out at paltry winter stars deep between huge gray clouds that hung on the sky like outer draperies, and Dan said, "I'm going to remember these early months of this year."

"Yes?"

"The time of the healing. Good God, what's been wrong with me?"

"One of those long things that just take time. Now you're snapping back. And you look it, Dan."

"Three months ago I was ready to go back to the sanitarium. One night I even telephoned. I was about to ask for Jo Drew. Who knows, she may still be there. But then I lost my courage and hung up."

"Jo Drew?" I had not heard the name before.

"Josephine Drew. A nurse. She did most for me when I was in that place. A wonderful girl."

"Oh, yes."

"Now I'd like to see her for other reasons, just as a person, because she is wonderful. I don't know why I haven't. You'd like her, Grant."

"Why haven't you seen her?"

"Sickness and pride, I guess. That's no doubt part of my whole miserable business. Have I seen anyone?"

"Well, do now."

"It's as though I'm just waking up," he said. Then suddenly he looked dubious. "I don't think Milly. . . ."

"Milly?"

"I'm not sure that they like each other."

Oh, what an innocent he had always been! "Milly knows her?" I asked.

"Slightly. And some years ago now, of course."

"They haven't seen each other either?"

"No, no. Why should they have seen each other?"

And then when Milly came in, breathless and surprised to find me already there, I said, after the greetings and the exclamations, "Dan's been telling me about Josephine Drew."

Nothing happened to her face. "Josephine Drew," she said, and then, glancing at Dan, "Oh, yes. Have you seen her, Dan?"

"No. I thought it might be pleasant if we did."

"Of course. But it's been so long—do you know where she is?"

"I hadn't thought—I haven't thought of her—I only thought—" Suddenly he was all uncertain again.

"We'll see, dear," Milly said briskly, and told us then, in some detail, how really mild it seemed for February. But when Freddie, looking very cheerful, came in a few minutes later, she said almost at once, "Freddie, Dan's been speaking of Josephine Drew. Do you remember her?"

His face did show something, it dulled somehow as he said, "Of course," and looked at me and at Milly again. Then there was nothing but a thick silence, while that glance between them held, until I said, "How did it go today, Freddie?" and he seemed to wake up abruptly and said, "Oh, fine, fine!"

And *fine, fine* seemed to provide the refrain that ran through dinner, at least for Dan and Freddie, as Dan, out of his new independence and Freddie out of the promise of his near success, babbled on together. I waited for another mention of Josephine Drew, but it did not come; she seemed, indeed, to have been forgotten by all of them, and I became aware, as the animation of the two men mounted with their wine, that Milly spoke less and less. She toyed with her food, turned her wineglass before her interminably but hardly touched her wine, and at last let her eyes rest on me where I sat opposite her, and then, moodiness suddenly falling away, smiled directly at me with a warmth not only of friendliness but even of affection such as I had not seen for months and that, at this moment, struck me as entirely unaccountable. Nor did I understand much more clearly when, after dinner, Dan and Freddie having withdrawn briefly to Dan's desk in another room, Milly and I were alone together and she made her extraordinary plea.

We were in the large, glassed-in room, staring at empty coffee cups and brandy glasses, and suddenly Milly got up and turned down the bright lights. I stood up, too, and then, without a word, she walked swiftly toward me and put her arms around my neck. "Love me," she said quietly and desperately. "Oh, love me again."

I gasped. "I do love you."

"No, no. You don't at all."

"But for months now, you've disliked me."

"Oh, no!" Her breath was on my neck, her moist cheek against my chin as she strained upward, weeping silently. "Don't let me do it, Grant, don't please."

"Do what, my dear?"

"Don't let me be worse!"

I was silent as I tried to understand her. "I'll do anything you want," I said.

"Then love me again, and let Freddie go."

"Freddie? How—let him go?"

"This silly magazine business. He'll be no good at that. Please—drop it."

"But he's quite good at it, really. And *he* doesn't want it dropped!"

"But I do. Do it for me, then, and love me again, so that I won't be worse than I am."

She sounded more desperate than I had ever heard her, and she was clinging to me with tense arms, and it was quite honestly that I said, "Milly, I don't understand you. Not at all."

She drew away a little and stared down at our feet. She wiped her eyes. Still looking down, she said, "Dan needs him so. Why do you insist?"

"But Dan demonstrably doesn't," I did insist. "It's good for both of them. Wonderful. Watch—it will *make* Dan."

She looked up at me again. There was a kind of dim pain in her eyes, but now no affection whatever for me. That had come and gone like a breeze. She said, "Oh!" with something like dismay, and then turned from me entirely and walked to the windows. The two men came back into the room, we sat down again round the chaste fire, and for the rest of that evening I was unable to engage her glance. Now she seemed intent only on Freddie.

The following Sunday was a mild, mild day, the truly false

spring, and there were still to be blizzards and gales before the real spring came, the city to be choked with snow; but for that day the air was soft as April, and in the middle of the afternoon Dan called to say that they were driving into the country for an early supper and would I come along. When they came for me, Freddie was driving and Milly sat beside him. I got into the back seat with Dan.

We crossed the Hudson and drove north; we found an inn; we dined. And there was nothing remarkable about that evening except that Milly, in considerable contrast to her behavior of a few nights before, seemed almost drunk with animation, but a false animation, electric and a little wild and meaningless. On the way back to the city, this mood sustained itself, and seemed to quiet rather than to animate the rest of us. When we passed an amusement park, garish with lights and splitting the night with its blaring sounds, Milly insisted that we stop. We wandered among the crowd that the mild evening had drawn. We found a shooting gallery with pistols, and we all bought a few rounds, but Milly, in her curious excitement, could hit nothing, whereas Dan, amid Milly's exclamations and Freddie's fulsome compliments, did best, and he did superbly, so that over and over he won another round, until the sheer skill of his performance became tiresome.

"Why, that's fine, Dan, that's fine!" Freddie said, as though he were encouraging an invalid in a long convalescence, and I said as bluntly as I could, "You're just as good as you always were, Dan. The only one of us who is."

"But let's go on!" Milly cried, and we went on, and found a Fun House. We crashed about through corridors of distorting mirrors, stumbled up and down shaking stairs, balked before jigging, phosphorescent skeletons that leapt up before us in dark rooms, and always led by Milly, as though this nonsense were a quest, on and on.

Then we came finally to a point near the exit where a smooth, enormous wooden saucer revolved crazily in the floor, first in one direction, then violently in the other. And although this pit already contained two sailors and two shrieking girls in wild disarray, their limbs all tangled and their bodies sprawling, Milly slid in among them, and Freddie after her. But almost at once something disastrous happened. She had miscalculated the thing somehow and injured herself. Freddie, struggling for a semblance of balance, was holding onto her and shouting to the man who manipulated the levers that operated the device. It ground to a sudden halt, and the sailors helped Freddie bring Milly out of it. She had hurt her ankle and her lip was swollen and bleeding, but she impatiently dismissed the operator, who was mildly concerned, and wanted nothing from Dan but his handkerchief. We helped her outside and started for the car, and although she could not put her weight on the injured foot, she continued to laugh. "It's nothing. I was just silly. It's nothing at all."

And it wasn't, really, and yet it was grotesque that it should have happened to her, and when we came to the car and Freddie brusquely ordered, "Grant, you drive. We'll put Milly in the back," she did, it seemed to me, sob once or twice even as she laughed. Freddie managed to arrange her as comfortably as possible on the back seat, with her back up against a window and her bruised leg stretched out along the seat. Then Dan said, "I'll sit with Milly," and Freddie replied, "But I'm already here, Dan. Why not leave it this way?" And indeed he was very substantially there, sitting on the edge of the seat, his arm around her shoulders to cushion them. Dan got in with me.

In the highway darkness, when there was no point in further expressions of concern, we all fell silent, and Dan's head drooped in a doze. There was little traffic, and I drove fast and intently. Occasionally I thought I heard whispering, murmurous sounds behind me, but I could not turn. At a traffic light, I took occasion to readjust the rearview mirror and said a word or two over my shoulder, and then we drove on again, fast and intently. But I heard those sounds again, tender and murmuring, and, without reducing our speed, I looked into the mirror as another car came toward us. In the flash of its headlights, I saw one of Milly's white hands on the dark cloth of Freddie's shoulder, and I saw his mouth on her cheek.

Now, when it was too late, I understood: she had become "worse," and my poor plot had been subverted.

It came to a rapid ruin. Only a few afternoons later, flushed and angry, Freddie lurched into my cubicle of an office and demanded, "Why did you do it?"

"Do what, Freddie?"

"Get me in here only to get me out. *Why?*"

I stood up. "What do you mean?"

"The inquisition I've been through."

"I don't know what you're talking about."

"Don't you!" His hands were shaking, and he put them on my desk, palms down, fingers spread out, to steady them, and, shoulders thrust toward me, he said in a moment, said slowly, "I don't think you ever did like me, Grant."

I came around the desk and took hold of his arm. "Freddie, be quiet. I'm not even going to pursue that. You're excited. Calm down and tell me what happened."

He drew his arm roughly out of my grasp. "Ask your editor," he said, and slammed out.

The editor was almost as angry as Freddie. "A nice spot you put me on," he said.

"What is this?"

"Did you know this fellow's politics?"

"I know *him*. He's not political at all."

"You've been around long enough to know that that usually means the worst politics."

"What happened?"

"This came in today," he said, and slid a sheet of notepaper across his desk. I read the few typewritten lines. *As an old friend of "The New World," I advise you to ask a few questions of Mr. Grabhorn before you employ him. Ask him, for example, for his opinion of Franco, of Chamberlain, of F.D.R., or ask him to give you his views of the idea of WPA art. Ask him, too, whether he has squeezed fine pictures out of helpless refugees for a small fraction of their worth.* That was all; there was no signature.

"A queer thing," I said. "You don't think it's mine, do you?"

"Yours? Of course not. But you must have known some of this."

"Did you let him think that I had anything to do with it?"

"No. That's what I'm complaining about—that you didn't."

"Well, he thinks I did. What happened?"

"I asked him, that's all. And found out. The fellow's a fascist. What did he think he was going to do on this magazine?"

"No, no. Now look—"

"Friendship blinds you, Grant."

"He's no great friend of mine, but I've known him for a long time, and I know what he's like, and I really thought that he could handle this job."

"So do I know what he's like—now. And we can't have a fellow like that on this staff!" Then, more patiently, he said, "You should have known that. Maybe you're too humane."

I smiled. "No. That isn't the problem. Well, I'm sorry. . . ." And I was.

Freddie never really believed me again. I thought at first that I had persuaded him of my innocence in that miserable *New World* affair, but I do not now think that he ever relinquished his suspicions, and in the end he was convinced that I had indeed indulged myself in that act which, from me, would have been an insanely perverse betrayal of his interests. The real source of that betrayal was, of course, plain enough to me, and there it was in the open for us now, a thing perfectly evident between us, like an object, a shadow or a sword, over which we stared at one another, both of us knowing now, neither, of course, yet speaking. But knowing: knowing on Milly's part that she had saved him from me; knowing on my part not only that I had failed to save her and Dan from him, for themselves, but also that for her there was logic in the act—insane logic, perhaps, but desperate logic, too (desperation, we finally learn, is almost more importunate than anything else)—a new and savage intensity and clarity in her determination to hold to herself what she had so fatally chosen as her life.

And still, in spite of this recognition, we went on for a few more months in a manner that seemed the same as before. There were cocktails, a concert or two, and an occasional invitation to dinner, maintaining the surface, and so I saw them five or six times at their apartment as that winter trailed to an end and we trailed on through the dreary fiction of a relationship that no longer existed. There was no more verbal dancing, nothing so flighty. Under the thin surface of that fiction everything was hostile and cold, and I maintained it only because of Dan, pitiable and shrunken, and tragically impervious.

The last time I saw them in that friendless establishment was in April. Freddie was again in charge of the household, as he was again fully engaged in the operations of the gallery, but things with him were not quite as they had been before, either.

When he gave up his short-lived but childishly bright dream of becoming the elegant critic-connoisseur, he gave up something else, too, something physically manifested; for while he was not exactly heavier, his body seemed more slack, as though there had been a general loosening up of all the strings and bobbins that held him together, as though, indeed, his little sortie into independence was a major fact for him, a crisis, a one-and-only effort that, failing, left him with something else which, perforce, he would for the rest of his life treasure as the best. Their new alliance was one which neither of them quite wanted and to which neither of them could rise with any fullness of intent, but it had its logic, too: it bound them finally, and it bound Dan in with them. And so, at the same time that he underwent a slump of spirit that seemed to show in his very walk, there had also been some tightening of the nerves, some narrowing of the will, as with Milly, and this came to me like a message from his brooding, hazel eyes whenever he let them fall upon me in his new distrust and his new security.

It was April twilight, and in that violet light his face seemed to glimmer as he handed me a highball. "Milly and Dan will be in right away," he said with some kind of mockery. "Sorry to keep you waiting. They did want to say good-by."

"Good-by?"

"Yes, good-by again. We're off once more."

"Where?"

"Spain." As though he had said Bermuda or Arizona. It was like a stab with a knife.

"Spain?"

"Dan needs a rest. We're closing the gallery early—until October. Needs redecoration anyway. And Dan needs to get out of New York. Needs to get away from this tension."

"So you chose Spain," I said.

"Wonderful country," he said with his curious new mockery. "Sun. Swimming. We can fish. Long motor trips. It will do just what Dan needs."

"Don't neglect to bait his hook," I said.

He looked at me with quick amusement and then said, solemnly, "No, of course not."

I wanted to hit him. I said, "Spain in the spring of *this* year for a peaceful vacation! Really, Freddie, who are you kidding?"

"No one. We've thought about it a good deal. Spain will be perfect for a month or two. Really, of course, it's Portugal we're interested in, and I'll be there most of the time."

"Portugal." I was not following him, except that he seemed still to be mocking me, and in the deepening light, blue now, his plangent features had taken on an evil glint.

"Lisbon," he said, his voice dropping toward a whisper of delight. "Lisbon. God, it's like a little door, almost the only one, almost the only hole out of Europe. And there they are, all of them, jammed up against it, trying to get out, having to get out as best they can, really willing to pay. Because, after all, it means their lives."

"And they have pictures?"

He grinned at me with brutal boyishness. "Of course. Old and new. Off their stretchers. Rolled-up canvases in briefcases and bags. Walking around with them under their arms. Looking for buyers." His elation made me turn away from him.

"You'll kill two birds," I said.

"Exactly. With one passage. This really is the moment to be there, the exact time, it couldn't be better."

"The squeeze has never been so tight?"

"Oh, we'll do well!" he said, and laughed. "And Dan, too. Let's have some light." And in a moment he transformed that dim blue well of a room, dug out of sky, into its characteristically cold brilliance. It was like a signal. For at that moment, Dan and Milly came in from the corridor that led to the bedrooms. Milly walked ahead, walked rapidly toward me in an ice-blue satin dress that clung to her heavy thighs as she moved and whose neck was slashed down to the midriff. She wore large, cobwebby earrings of brilliants, and her hair, which seemed nearly white, was pulled up on her head and pushed forward and held there by some sort of flashing jeweled clasp. No simple blue flower now! Her hand in mine was as cold as she looked, and before I had even really seen Dan behind her, there flashed into my mind—perhaps because of that silly conversation about goddesses that we had had not very long before, and because the subject now was so much more relevant —into my mind that passage from *Ulysses*, where the hallucinatory nymph loftily addresses Bloom as follows: "We immortals, as you saw today, have no such place and no hair there either. We are stone cold and pure. We eat electric light. . . ." and poor Bloom, in a new abjectness, paces the heath and declares, "O, I have been a perfect pig!" Then I looked at Dan and saw that the application did not extend to him. He looked merely, thoroughly ill.

"Hello, darling! Sorry we were late. But Freddie's taken care of you, hasn't he?"

"Freddie always does. How magnificent you're looking."

She took my nearly empty glass. "Freddie," she said, and held it out to him without taking her eyes from me. They rested on me with a blue, distant blankness, and I felt my own eyes dim over in a spasm of sorrow. "Dan," I said to escape that empty look, and reached around Milly to take his hand. "I'm glad that you're getting away."

"I guess I need to," was all that he said, and in his dark eyes there was another emptiness, a trance of terror.

"We all need to," Milly interposed. "Freddie has some wonderful business to do, and I've come to the stage where a winter in New York undoes me." Her silly artificiality was like a wall of glass between us, and held off on my side of it, my heart trembled with pity for her. Could I have saved her? I think not. For when she begged, "Love me again," that is not quite what she had meant. And still, remembering that dim afternoon in the vast drawing room of the old Ford apartment when I told her that I loved her, I remembered too her small lost figure in the shadows, and I knew that now, in the hard role that she had found for herself, she was truly lost, the girl gone forever and no woman born. "Ah, thank you, Freddie," she cried, and took two glasses from his tray, one very light, and gave the heavier one to Dan. I took another, Freddie the fourth, and then we sat down, and it was as if they were all waiting for me to talk. But what was there to talk about?

Only their plans. So I asked, "Aren't there any restrictions on travel in Spain? Right now, one would think—"

Freddie broke in. "No. Why should there be? After all, for a change we showed the unusual good sense to stay out of an affair that was none of our business."

I checked my anger. "Of course. But a country just out of war—I'd suppose—"

"Spain?" Milly asked mildly, and looked from me to Freddie and back again.

"Well, restrictions or not, I don't understand it," I said, "I don't understand you."

"Why not?" Freddie asked promptly.

"You want to give Dan a rest, get him out of tensions, and you take him to a country that's just been torn in two, where the blood must still be running, political murders going on at a mass rate—"

Dan shuddered in his chair, and "What are you talking about?" Milly asked angrily.

Freddie laughed. "I'm sorry," he said. "I've been trying to get a rise out of Grant, that's all. I told him we were going to

Spain. Of course, we're not, Grant. Your convictions make you gullible. We *are* going to Portugal. And to France. Marseilles is another of those doors."

I felt myself flush, and now, I thought, I'd let them have it, *my* knowledge, and I said, "Very funny. Really, if you want to give Dan a rest, why don't you two go abroad alone and leave him with me?"

Each of them jerked a little, each except Dan, who only lifted his eyes to me and smiled wanly.

"Are you serious?" Milly asked with a stiff laugh.

"Why not?"

"Oh, for God's sake!" said Freddie.

In anger I had taken that plunge and now I was unwilling to climb back. "Why not?" I repeated. "Dan, you let them plan too much for you." I was looking only at him, refusing to accept their signals of eye and mouth. "Why do you? Do you want to go on this expedition? Or is it only that Milly and Freddie feel you should? How long since you've made any plans for yourself?"

"They plan well," he said quietly, with a tremor of agitation in his voice.

"We plan together," Milly said. "Will you be kind enough not to interfere?"

I caught the blue blaze of her look. "I'm making a friendly suggestion," I said, "and quite seriously. If Dan needs looking after, I'd be only too delighted."

"What nonsense!" Freddie exploded. "Of course, Dan wants to go. We wouldn't want to go without him. We're going primarily on business, and there'd be no point in going at all without the benefit of Dan's judgment."

"Ah yes," I said, "Dan's judgment."

Freddie put his glass down with a thump. "Well?" he demanded as he rose to his feet.

"How long since you've let Dan use it?" I asked, looking up at him.

"Grant," Milly said with slow deliberateness, "will you please—"

Dan giggled. "What a funny quarrel," he said. "What's it about?"

I stood up. "What indeed?"

"We're not quarreling, dear," Milly said, as if he were a child.

Then Freddie made the really preposterous remark. "If only you could get a decent long vacation sometime, Grant, and come with us. That would be the solution."

"Yes," said Milly quickly in a weird imitation of pleasure. "That would be!"

They were hoisting me back up on the safe shelf of our usual conversational inanities, and when poor, simple Dan said, "Wonderful idea! Can't you, Grant, this time? Can't you try?" it was clear that I was back up there, and for the moment I could only smile.

"I'm afraid not, not this time," I said. And it was almost as if the very room gave forth a sigh of relief.

"We'll think of you in the hot New York summer," Milly said.

"Pity me. Well, I must be going."

"Already?"

But I was not quite ready. Half way out I stopped and said as casually as I could, "Queer business about that French boat, isn't it?"

"French boat?"

"The *Paris*. Bringing the French art over for the Fair."

"What art?" Dan asked. "What boat?"

Milly laughed. "Grant, you must spend all your time reading newspapers."

"A good deal of it."

Freddie brushed by me on his way to the vestibule, and Dan asked, "What art?"

"A number of pictures were destroyed by fire on this boat—"

"Nothing at all serious," said Milly.

"I'm interested," I persisted, "in the way that, try as you may to keep them separate, even art and political violence get mixed up."

"An accident," Milly said firmly.

"What happened?" from Dan.

I was aware of Freddie behind me, and in a moment he was helping me into my coat. I said, "No, it wasn't an accident. They're holding an Italian workman for sabotage. The fascists didn't want that ship to get over here. And besides the damage to the pictures—" Freddie was positively shaking me into my coat and I tried not to smile as I finished "—besides the damage the fire did to the pictures, a number of men were killed."

Silence, and then, from Dan, in a whisper, "Killed?"

"I'll walk out with you," Freddie said. "I have an errand to do before dinner."

"Good-by, Grant," Milly said, giving me her hand with a smart thrust.

"*Bon voyage!* And do get a rest, Dan."

He looked at me with a dim stare, and as Freddie led me out of there by the arm, I looked back over my shoulder, and I wanted to cry it out loudly now, *Dan, you poor, blind baby, what preposterous thing are you letting them do to you?*

Outside in the street again, in the soft gray evening, where the air was large and the vistas long, it was possible to believe that one was sane. Yet Freddie was walking beside me with a deliberate tread, off on some errand that was a clear invention, and while he was there, the madness from which I had just been plucked trailed me still. I did not propose to help him bring out whatever sentiments weighed upon him, and we walked in silence. We had gone a long block and turned west into a crosstown street before he began. Then he began mildly enough. "You can see how really sick Dan is."

"Yes, I can."

"You might be more helpful."

"You didn't start me off very helpfully, with that nonsense about Spain."

"I'm sorry. That was a bit of self-indulgence, and I am sorry. But that was my fault, not theirs, and you might have spared Milly, not to say Dan."

"Did I harm them?"

"You don't seem to recognize Milly's worth. What sort of wreck do you think Dan would be now if it weren't for her?"

"Worse?"

He snorted impatiently. "Good God, if you had known what he *was!* A walking dead man. Even Milly and I—we were like shadows to him, he hardly knew we were there. Then the sanitarium. The people there did a lot for him. He has his ups and downs now, needs still, of course, a kind of constant protection, needs rest and a reasonable freedom from responsibility, and all this Milly gives him. I told you before, it was his marriage that saved him."

"It was so quick, wasn't it?" I said blandly.

He glanced at me closely from under the brim of his hat, and he said, "No quicker than it had to be. She married him to save him."

"You mean she didn't really love him?"

"Love him? Certainly she loved him."

"I mean—" Then I found myself fumbling for words, almost ashamed under his blank stare, which was intended, it seemed, to make me feel that I was uttering obscenities.

"What *do* you mean?"

"Yes—what? Love. What does *it* mean?"

"I suppose she always loved him. But her marriage—there was more in that than anything that there had been before."

"Did you know their plans?"

He gave me that close look again. "No, I didn't. When I knew about it, they were married. In a way, there was an element of self-sacrifice there, and Milly had the grace not to want that question raised or discussed. And she was right." We had come to Third Avenue, and at a corner, nearly under the elevated tracks, he stopped and said, "She was right because it was their marriage that brought him back to life."

"You mean, Freddie, that life we've just come from up there? Is that life at all? Good God!"

A neon sign, flashing nearby, turned his face savage red and gray by turns as he stared at me, and I could not see what anger was gathering there, or what was pulsing in his weirdly gleaming eyes. But suddenly he had hold of my arms in a terrific grip, and his fantastic, straining face was nearly touching mine. "You keep out of this!" he shouted. "*We're* his friends. *We* know what he needs. *We* love him! Get that straight, and from now on, *you keep out of this!*"

There had been no transition. Anger had blown up like a wind, mine no less than his. I wrenched my arms free and shoved him violently against the building behind him. "Get your filthy hands—" I started, but did not finish, for he recovered himself at once and he had seized the front of my coat at the chest in one fist, and was drawing back the other. We were reenacting, with the same unreasoning and undefined anger, that attic scene of our boyhood. Only it came to me suddenly that we were not boys, and that he was something of a buffoon, and I began to laugh. "Don't be an ass, Freddie," I said. "You wouldn't hit me."

Two or three curious spectators had gathered around us. He glanced at them, then let go of my coat and let his fist drop. It had all taken less than half a minute. We stared at each other. I laughed again. I had an impulse to forgive him for everything.

The stragglers drifted away, and suddenly Freddie turned and started back in the direction from which we had come. Then I wanted to call to him. "Freddie, come back! For God's sake, let's be men!" I wanted to call. But I did not, and I watched his implacable back as it disappeared among others.

Then an unpleasant experience came over me. There, among all the slam-bang of traffic, among all the street noises, the horns, the shouting, the laughter, under the sudden horrible clatter of a train overhead, among the hundreds of human beings who were surging up and down the sidewalks—in the throbbing heart of the city, I was suddenly alone; there seemed, quite simply, quite horribly, to be no one else in the world.

5

The rest comes in glimpses. It occurred in the months that followed on the Pact, the months of the invasion of Poland and the beginnings of the phoney war, and it comes now in glimpses, small-shuttered, sometimes spectacular, glimpses of madness and of a mad unwinding. To the small events, the large times were appropriate; we seemed, indeed, to be playing some odd miniature shadow game with history. And in the phantasmagoria of history, with all that chaos of clumsy alliances and shattering events, my private phantasmic isolation grew. It played its small part in the disaster of these others.

When we are very close to things in time, there is little likelihood of our handling them like artists. We summon up no recollections in tranquillity; what we summon up is what we are still living, what has not yet passed through the sieve of time that true recollection demands, has not arranged itself in the mysterious mind into that core of the essential which in itself is the selective process that enables the artist, finally, to think he chooses to tell what he will tell. Now, in this present and of that near past, I tell everything. And in a sense, that everything, which is very brief, *is* an essence, or at least an ultimate of all that has gone before. I omit only what pertains to me alone as apart from these others—my work, of course, and its slow deterioration, but also my attempt to find in various women a life, an attachment. Only one of those attempts, the most real, the only desperate one, pertains at all, and of that one I will have to tell although it, too, can be briefly told.

But first—I find, as I approach the end, that I am reluctant to come to it. If we remember too much, we risk madness; if we remember too little, we are probably fools. Remembering with measure, we are artists, supposing that there is also measure to remember. And measure is what—my reiterated effort to tell this story as I wish to tell it is proving, I begin to feel, in vain again—measure is what that situation was without. Excess, excess! And finally catastrophic misery. And my own buckling under the design that I have meant you to have, the design itself buckling somewhere. Where? Let me finish the story and perhaps we shall see.

That autumn was intolerable, melancholy like many another autumn, but worse, much worse, as I found myself constantly on the verge of sinking into that nightmare in which I seemed to be abstracted from the universe, an experience that was almost visual in that the objects that made up the world around me, people, buildings, the walls of a room, seemed just to recede a little, to pull away from me into a kind of static isolation, leaving me there in the center, totally out of touch somehow, without relation! In this mood, I thought naturally and often of those three. They must be back, I said to myself in September, in October, and occasionally I would wander past their apartment building, staring up to their turret of glass to see if there were lights, but it was too high and set back besides and I could never tell; so sometimes I would stand on Fifty-seventh Street opposite The Ford Gallery, waiting for one or another of them to come or go, but they did not. This was perhaps all on my own account, a desire to get back to a point before Freddie's street-corner challenge, before Milly's last plea to me and her consequent final sacrifice of herself, and to try again to have them as friends. Or I would remind myself that, after all, Freddie was not Dan, or even Milly, and then, quite apart from my own needs, the thought of Dan preyed upon me, a young man still who might be a brilliant success in the world but who was being victimized by an insane love and held out of the world. And now I did not think of Freddie and Milly as at all vicious. If vice consists of a recognition of base motives, they were never vicious. I thought of them as mistaken, sadly mistaken, and pitied them, for, suffering themselves from a certain blindness to the truly inescapable conditions of modern life, they were always able to say to themselves with complacency, "*We're* his friends. *We* know what he needs. *We* love him!" and pursue his destruction with the most exalted notions of tenderness and virtue. And Dan himself could so easily assist in the collaboration. Bred as he was in that atmosphere of Bohemian-aristocratic detachment, and having both by that breeding and his own temperamental bias the old-fashioned aesthete's aloofness from the hard run of ordinary things, he made his own protected isolation easy. Freddie's aestheticism was of another kind. Freddie was tough in will, and his was a chosen role, active and deliberate, the mask of a narrow soul. These reflections encouraged me finally, in November, to risk Freddie's not very formidable wrath and try once more for Dan's sake.

I telephoned Dan at the gallery and asked him whether I could pick him up for lunch. He seemed surprised and pleased and then said, "But Freddie's not here, he's out with a client."

"Well, you and I alone, then," I said. "All the better."

His hesitation suggested that this was a strange idea, but presently he said, "All right. Fine. Come on over when you can."

I went early in the hope that Freddie would not have returned, and yet I felt a little trepidation as I entered that chic foyer, with its black and white parquetry, on either side an elegant Regency bust of marble on a garlanded column, and as I went up the stairs into the first room. There were two men there, in overcoats, standing in conversation before some Matisse flowers.

"In French painting," one of them was saying, "the background is part of the picture. In American"—and he swung round a little to point at a Milton Avery that hung opposite—"it is nothing, background only."

"Good teachers," the other murmured. "Monet. . . ."

"You see how he knows that the background should be broken up, like that, then brought into the front—? That other? Flowers in a teapot."

I went up three or four more steps to a further room. There a young woman was busy at a small desk. "Mr. Norman?" she asked. "Mr. Ford's expecting you." She opened two large doors into the private showroom, and there was Dan, slumped on a sofa.

Even before he stood up to greet me, I saw that he was worse. He looked older, but not in experience, only in an invalided way, shrunken, really, his eyes dim, the skin on his face loose, his mouth drawn, much grayer. And when he was on his feet, I saw that he had become a little stooped, so that he looked smaller. "We thought that you'd given us up again," he said with a quaver.

"No, no," I muttered, unable to bring myself to ask him how he was.

And I did not need to, for without any preamble, he said, "I've not been well, Grant. Not at all well."

"I'm sorry, Dan."

He moved to a cabinet and found some glasses and whisky, and over the fizz of the soda, he said to the muffled wall, "I don't know what to do."

We sat down together on the sofa. "I want to help. There must be something that can be done, something that I can do."

"Everything upsets me. . . ."

"Such as what?"

"Anything at all." His voice was petulant. "Anything."

"Well, Dan, the world now is enough to give us all bad nerves." I was thinking of the air stiff with the threat of bombs about to plummet down on great cities, of the doors to the West closing one after another, of Europe in flames, and America . . . ?

He looked at me blankly. "I don't mean that. Little things —a rude waiter last night. . . . Stupid things!"

"Oh." Momentarily, I wondered why I was troubling with him. "Your summer's rest didn't help?"

"No. And I was no help to them, to Milly and Freddie. They had to do all the work." Suddenly he put his drink down on the floor and clenched his hands together and bent over them in a spasm. "God, it's awful," he said. "At night now, I wake up, I see them, I hear them screaming."

"Them?"

"It gets worse, it gets worse. As if I had only that one thing in my life."

"What thing?"

"That one memory, of my mother, my father," he said bleakly.

"Ah, yes, yes," I said quickly. "Terrible! Only wait—even such horrors fade finally."

"But no!" he cried, leapt up, walked a step or two, came back, and sat down again. "No. It doesn't. That's what unnerves me. It *grows* instead. It's always there. And now, I tell you, at night—and at night it's the worst, the clearest! It grows and grows, and it's all I have. . . ."

"But it's not all you have. You have this gallery. You have your whole life ahead of you. You have your marriage. Milly's so thoughtful, so competent—surely she's helped." I paused.

"But what does keep it alive then, over so long a time?"

He stood up and hitched nervously across the room. He stood with his back to me for a moment, a small figure in that tall room entirely hung with dark gray draperies except for one end of the room, where room-tall hinged screens for pictures stood, as in a museum storeroom, a kind of giant metal file at the edges of which Dan now seemed to be staring. When he turned around he said, "Of course, Milly's been wonderful, and Freddie, too, for all the rest of it, all that she couldn't manage. What would I be without Milly? I wouldn't be here at all, I imagine. My only luck in a long time, I guess, was that I didn't marry that other girl, who couldn't possibly have been as patient, as—"

"Other girl, Dan?"

He looked at me in surprise that I did not know about her. It was characteristic of his present self-engrossment that he should have assumed that I did. "I told you, Jo Drew, the nurse at Windhaven. I told you how fine she was, and how I nearly called her last winter." He paused and his eyes darkened, and then he smiled ruefully, rather attractively in the old way, and he finished, "I owe her a great deal, but most, I guess, for throwing me over. And that's why I couldn't bring myself to ask for her when I called."

That was Milly's luck, not his, I thought, but I could only say, "You told me about her, but not that you wanted to marry her."

"Well, I did, for a while," he said, but the faint regret of his smile was gone, and he was smiling again with the tense, humorless egotism that was more usual with him.

"Do you see a doctor?" I asked.

"Doctors can't help me," he said. "There's nothing wrong with me that they can help. It's only that picture that comes all the time. It's here." He put his hand on his forehead.

"There are such doctors."

"They can't help that."

"They did once, didn't they, at Windhaven?"

"I can't go back there now."

"Why not?"

"I can't."

"Why not?"

"I've got to live through this myself."

"That's silly, Dan."

He changed the subject. "We had wonderful luck in Europe," he said with a kind of animation. "It's a grab bag now, you know. I'd like to show you some of the things we brought back. Especially three pieces that a German was trying to get off his hands. But we have to keep them under cover for a while. There's always the danger of their being loot. Although Freddie, who dug these up, is very good at such business, and especially if there's a little intrigue involved, very good, very circumspect. Intrigue fascinates him, makes him sharper than ever. He made friends with these people, and after that—"

As I watched him across the expanse of room and only half-listened to his prating, my mind was running on its own course. I began to understand now how Milly's vanity (or Milly's fear?) had worked, extraordinary compulsion that it was. Josephine Drew, even though in the end she had been unwilling to marry Dan, must yet have made it clear to Milly that she would lose Dan to someone unless she married him herself. And I thought that now I understood why their marriage had been so quick, so quiet. And Freddie?

That was different. I had now only one desire for myself, and that was to find a woman to whom my commitment could be complete, to find a relationship knit with those details of responsibility in the very minor, daily things as in the major, moral ties—in short, a marriage; and out of the very intensity of that desire I began now to understand Freddie more clearly than I had before. He was that kind of perennial bachelor who, although often attractive to women and needing to be intimately in their company, is yet pathologically incapable of marriage. Some deeply childish irresponsibility unfits them for just those minute and multitudinous strands of responsibility which this most demanding and most rewarding of human relationships exacts and which a marrying man wants. Often the unmarrying man attaches himself, then, as "best friend" to some household in order to come as close as possible to the thing which he is incapable of seizing in itself. In a queer and intense way, Freddie was one of those, and of *his* marrying, or even, except for his single attempt, of straying from her, Milly never had to worry, least of all now, when she had given him more than he had ever intended to ask for, and had taken finally all that there was of him.

And then, as with Dan, there was that childhood thing again. In human affairs, the background is the picture. Freddie had been the outsider, the village boy who found us attractive when most of his townsmen resented the summer colony, to whom—perhaps for the very reason that he came into our life on sufferance, and that by allying himself with us he cut himself off from his true allegiances—the group came to mean more than it ever did to me or, I think, to Dan.

Dan's tragedy lay in his passivity, in his terrible capacity to *accept*. It was as if he were material devised to be worked upon by the aggressive will of others, their frenetic loyalties. For Milly and Freddie were alike in that they were not jealous of individuals, as Freddie's long placidity in the face of Milly's marriage showed, but jealous, rather, for the narrow integrity of the group which together they comprised. Did they recognize that if the group relationship were to be kept intact, Dan must be deliberately sacrificed to it and their own persons exhausted by it at last? *"We're* his friends. *We* know what he needs. *We* love him!" they told themselves, and believed, I think, what they said. That they were unaware of their true motives does not exculpate them, of course, but it explains why, in the end, it was Dan alone of the three who saw the hideous truth for what it was.

He had stopped talking and was staring at me in a vacant way across the room. I finished my drink, put down my glass, and asked, "Shall we go?"

He awoke from his dazed abstraction and looked at his watch. "Milly ought to be along in a minute," he said.

"Oh, Milly's coming?"

"She's eager to see you. So I called her after you called. She'll be right along."

And in a moment she came. She entered briskly, in full and splendid sail, her heels tapping smartly across the uncarpeted floor. "Grant!" She put just the tips of her trimly gloved fingers into my hand. "You're so abrupt, my dear. You might have given me a little warning, just a little," she said with arch satire. Then she stepped past me and kissed Dan lightly on the cheek, as if he were a habit.

I stared at her. She looked as though she had just been taken out of the window of a shop, perfectly groomed, very beautiful in an exaggerated way, and utterly without feeling in her face.

"You like it?" she cried. "You approve?"

"What?"

"My coat, silly! It's new." She turned slowly to let me see it—sleek, gorgeous mink. "It's my birthday present from Dan and Freddie."

"Oh, yes. Very handsome."

"I've found," she said with an appalling sweetness, "that

you do much better if you can persuade men to give you things together." Her laughter was brittle and unembarrassed, and I felt blood rise to my face in a rush.

"I'll be with you in a minute," Dan said as he started for a door.

"Hurry, then," Milly called. "Freddie's holding a table for us."

"Oh, you found him?"

"Yes."

"Freddie, too," I said as Dan closed the door behind him.

She looked at me with faint scorn. "We don't do things separately, Grant. You know that."

"Nothing?"

"Nothing important."

"Is this important, this lunch?"

She hesitated. "I hope that Freddie and I aren't spoiling your plans."

I caught myself about to say "I'm delighted," or some other such casual lie, and for a moment I said nothing at all. Then, "I haven't any plans."

She smiled severely. "That's good. I thought perhaps you had. One never knows."

There are grim moments in all our lives when the progress of our fate appalls us, knocks us over, moments when we are suddenly made to see ourselves exactly where and as we are in what can be the grotesque stream of human relationship. This was such a moment, and as it seized hold of me, I felt my being groan, and I seized her hands. "Oh, my God, Milly, don't go on, please, don't let *us* go on."

"Go on?" she said faintly, as if my seizure had seized her, and did not take her hands away.

"How could this have happened?" I begged her. "Good God—consider what, all our lives, we *were*."

"Yes," she said, still in the faint voice, and suddenly she seemed small and human, vulnerable and entirely lovable. "I always consider that."

"Then, now, let's stop."

"What?"

"This."

"What?"

"What we're becoming, what we've become. You, a thousand miles away, and a thousand miles away from yourself."

"And you?"

I hesitated. "You asked me, a year ago, to love you. I failed. Let me love you now, in any way you say, any way you want."

She wavered. Her eyes looked out at me as if for trust. Her arms were trembling, even as I tightly gripped her hands. "Let me help you," I said.

She closed those eyes and she shuddered. "Ah, you can't help me now. You can't—and sometimes I think that this is all I've really learned in my life—you can't even help yourself."

I dropped her hands, I felt myself flush again, with anger now, and now my arms were trembling. Too loudly then, I said, "What in God's name is your game, Milly?"

"That's not an attractive word."

"The thing that's happening is not attractive, either. What are you two trying to *do?*"

"There are three of us."

"You two against Dan. Why?"

Her eyes flashed. "Don't be childish!"

I made myself speak calmly. "It's you who are childish," I said. "Don't you see it? Childish to the point of villainy. Don't you know it?" I put my hand on her sleeve. "Don't you know it, Milly?"

She moved away from me with a sharp gesture of dislike in

her shoulders. "Dan's sick, and I'm his wife, and Freddie's his friend—"

"His friend," I broke in. "And your—"

Her angry gray-blue eyes were like a seal, they stopped my mouth. "My?" she challenged me.

I waited, I let her feel her strength, before I finished, and finished with lame logic, "His friend can be your lover?"

How neatly then she turned the question away, as now she let herself smile upon me with slow, superior pity. "You can really ask that? You who don't know what love is? We do. And we have only one purpose, and that's to protect Dan, to get him well again. Is that a game?"

"Protect him from what, for heaven's sake?" I cried.

"From disaster. He's known one disaster that almost destroyed him—"

"But that's just it. You've cut him off from everything else. You've imprisoned him with that disaster. It's all he's got. He says so. It will ruin him utterly."

I had been speaking warmly, and she said, "You're excited," as she stared at me with unperturbed eyes. This enraged me. I moved to her swiftly and gripped her arms in their expensive fur, and without quite intending it, I began to shake her. "Listen to me!" I cried. "For God's sake, listen! You're unfitting him for everything, most of all for the ghastly truth!" I shook her.

"Let me go!" she said sharply.

"You've got to see, Milly. You've got to be *made* to see. How you and Freddie—"

Her voice rose. "You bungling, treacherous fool!"

Then I heard Dan behind me. "Grant!" he cried in a voice that was shrill with terror. I let Milly's arms drop and looked round.

"Oh, Dan!" Milly sobbed.

His face was white and he was shaking, hanging on to one of those tall frames for support. "Get out, Grant," he said. "Get out. Get out."

For a moment I wanted to laugh, for nothing else could have expressed my feeling for the outrageous excess in which we were there involved. But I did not laugh. I snatched up my coat and hat and started out. Yet I paused at the door. I turned to protest. When I saw that Milly had collapsed in Dan's weak arms, that, superb irony, he was ostensibly comforting *her*— then I knew, for the first time, the full extent of his terrible dependence. There is that horrible thing in nature, the embrace of spiders.

I did what I should have done long before: I sought out Josephine Drew. And if this were my story rather than theirs, what follows now would have to be a long interlude. When I found her, I said, "I didn't expect to find you," and I meant two things, meant not only that after so many years, four or five, it must have been, she might very probably not have been there at Windhaven any longer, but meant also that it had begun to seem unlikely that I would find in this world the woman that I needed. And what I knew almost at once was that this was she.

She was still there, for one reason, because her advancement on the staff had been rapid and she was no longer a nurse but, in effect, the resident director of the establishment. So I met a woman, that first time, dressed not in a white uniform as I had expected, but in a smart, highly tailored suit, and a woman who gave an immediate impression not of efficiency but of deep human warmth, whose entire *ambiente* was a rich and somehow serious sympathy. She was beautiful, but her beauty was not of feature alone; it seemed to be informed by the spirit of a clear and lovely intelligence that gave it candor, a profound candor. You will see why, in my mood, I was lost to her.

Yet the curious thing is that, physically, in a superficial way, she was not unlike Milly, or, at least, shared in the type of Milly's beauty. She had much the same stature, the same easy grace of movement that an earlier Milly had, and her face had the same structure of forehead, cheekbones, and jaw, the same triangular modeling. But her mouth was generous, and her eyes were brown, and her hair brown to auburn, so that, whatever the resemblance, the effect was of a quite different woman. As she was. They were like the good and wicked sisters of folklore. And thinking of Dan's attraction to this woman and his later marriage to Milly, I could not help speculating on the curious singleness of our impulses, by which felicity and doom can be so closely bound together, that narrow margin of choice between them to which our own inclinations limit us.

I told her a little about myself, of my relationship to Dan, and said that I had come on his account. She met his name with interest, even with pleasure, but as I began to tell her about his present condition, her warm expectancy turned to surprise.

"But that's awful," she said. "He left here in nearly perfect shape. Why—he was fine, he had really come through wonderfully! I can't believe—"

We sat in a waiting room on the second floor of the sanitarium, our chairs pulled up before an enormous window, and we looked out, over the Sound, to the open wintry sea. For a moment, she kept her eyes on the breakers crashing over a distant point of rock, white spume on the gray. Then she looked at me again and said, "Of course, in that time, many things could have happened. What did happen?"

"Nothing, particularly," I said. "Weren't the terms on which he was released rather strict for a nearly well man?"

"Terms? Strict? Were they?"

"His wife told me, when I first saw them again—and Dan seems to agree—that she was more or less under orders to protect him."

"From what?"

"From every kind of shock, from knowledge of even the most ordinary kind of violence and suffering."

"I don't understand you."

"For example. They keep newspapers away from him, and—"

I broke off because she looked so bewildered. At last she said, "His wife was overzealous. I remember that Dr. Cardigan said that he mustn't work too hard at first, that he ought to be relieved of any unusual burdens for a time, you know, that he should take things easy, as any convalescent should— All that, of course. But what you describe—it sounds like a continuing asylum."

"Yes," I said, and as I told her more of Dan's life, of that shelter that Milly and Freddie provided, her dismay grew. "I could cry!" she said softly at last, and her eyes were, as a matter of fact, dim, and then with a beautiful simplicity, she added, "I valued him."

"I know."

"They've undone everything, then."

"He must be made to come back here," I said.

She glanced at me. "Has he suggested that he might?"

"He's thought of it, I know. But his wife seems to feel that her care is sufficient, and now he seems to think so, too."

"Can you persuade him?"

"I'm afraid not."

"But he'd have to come voluntarily."

"Yes, and he would, I think, if *you'd* persuade him."

She started. "I?"

"Yes."

She looked at her hands in her lap. "But that's impossible,"
she said. "Not only for ethical reasons, although those exist,
too. But how could I go to him and not be misunderstood?"

"You won't?"

"I can't."

And by then I knew that I did not much want her to, at
least, just then. I did not want her to become involved with
them. And I said—I confess it—I said, instead of urging her,
"I understand. Perhaps I can get hold of him, although I don't
at this moment quite see how, under the circumstances."

"You'll try?"

"Yes." I hesitated. Then awkwardly I asked, "Tell me, are
you free to see me?"

"Free? Why not?"

"Good. Then can we have dinner tomorrow? In the city?"

She said that she would be charmed. And I let three months
pass while I pursued her.

I did not see the others, and I did not want to, nor, now, did
I want Jo to see them, for that, I felt, might somehow involve
the risk of my losing her. She kept a room in a small residence
hotel in town where she spent about half her nights, and so it
was easy for me to be with her. And this time, love and need
were so real for me that they disarmed me totally. I behaved
like an awkward boy who is too shy to attempt his first
kiss, agonizingly as he wants it, and yet, when I was not
with her, I suffered from a more drastic agony of loneliness,
that sense of being outside. For those few months, our relationship was that of friends, and from this woman, for whom intelligence counted, who had a deep interest in ideas and events
and a passionate devotion to human character, it seemed to me
most probable that only out of friendship could love come. In

that friendship, meanwhile, I had discovered the basis of the relationship that I needed now above all else.

I did not see the others, and when Jo asked occasionally, "What of Dan Ford?" I would explain again that since he had ordered me out of the gallery, and Freddie and Milly had both made it clear that they would prefer no further intrusions from me, I was delaying until some plausible opportunity enabled me to go there, or some accident threw us together. I did want Jo to go to Dan, for I felt that she could persuade him where I could not, but I did not want her to go until she was mine or had promised to be.

Then a curious circumstance forced my hand. Late in February, in the middle of an afternoon, as I was walking toward Fifth Avenue on Fiftieth Street, I saw Dan come toward me. He was running. He wore no hat, his hair was white, and his hands clutched his coat around him because his arms were not in the sleeves. His face was gray and his horrified eyes were staring far beyond me. "Dan! Dan!" I shouted as he passed me. I turned. He was still running. Then he stopped and for one long moment stared back at me, the eyes wide with panic, his mouth open. "Dan, wait!" I called. But he did not wait. He turned again and ran more quickly, with his coat slipping awkwardly off one shoulder, and then turned a corner onto Madison Avenue. I ran after him. When I came to the corner, he was no longer in sight. Where he had gone, what he was doing there, and why he was running, I had no idea, but quite clearly events had taken some ghastly turn.

That night I told Jo, and I begged her now to go to Dan.

"It sounds dreadful. But how can I? I *have* pride, damn it!"

"But pride isn't really involved, Jo, is it? And really, he's beyond misunderstanding your motives. He'll have no interest in them!"

"I don't want to be stubborn about it, or self-important. I

would like to help him. But it's not easy to divide yourself, as you seem to think I can."

"Divide yourself?"

"Yes. The friend-nurse, on the one hand, who has only the interests of a former patient at heart, and then, on the other, well, don't you see, *damn it*—the jilted bride?"

"What?"

"Isn't that what it comes down to?"

"How?"

She looked at me with that beautiful candor. "You know what happened, don't you? I thought you did, since you knew about me at all. You seemed to understand why I couldn't very well go to him."

"But, Jo, Dan didn't break that off!"

"Of course he did," she said quietly.

"But Dan told me that *you*—"

"Then he lied," she said promptly, and was silent. Then a long, frightful pause seemed to swell out in the silence like a thing, until at last she broke it with a kind of awful thoughtfulness in her voice. "Perhaps he didn't lie."

"Dan doesn't lie," I said.

"You mean—" And now she looked at me with horror.

"Yes."

Then *that* came out. We were sitting at a restaurant table facing each other, and while she spoke, she looked straight at me, and in the middle of her story I reached out and took her hand where it lay on the table. She told me quite directly, very simply, how on one April evening, as they were walking together through the grounds of the sanitarium, they had discovered and declared their love, and how, after that, in only a few weeks, Dan seemed completely well. Their plans were to be married immediately, as soon as a satisfactory substitute could be found for Jo at the sanitarium. Jo herself telephoned

Milly to come for Dan, and she came in her car to take him back
to the city. They told her together of their plans, and she seemed
very happy for them, and then she took Dan away. Two days
later Milly came again, with Freddie, and Freddie sat beside her
silently as Milly talked. She took Jo's hand and told her to be
brave, and she wept gently with her as she gave her the message which Dan—"poor, dear Dan"—was not man enough to
bring her himself: he asked to be released from his promise,
which he felt had come largely from his gratitude, for now,
away from the sanitarium, he found that he could not, after all,
marry her. And surely, Milly argued, it was better that Jo should
discover this weakness of character, this indecisiveness, then, before it was too late. . . . Oh, Milly was plausible! And Freddie said: "We've known him all our lives. He's impulsive, he's
generous to a fault, he's our best friend, but he is not, Miss
Drew, strong!"

"And then," I said, "she must have gone to him—from
you."

She stared at me. "I was five years younger then. I had never
been so hurt. And I was poor, and he was rich. And yet I thought
that I should not let it go that way. Not that I didn't believe
her. I did—completely. But for *his* sake. I felt that I should
make him face me. But I was hurt, and I couldn't. And my
whole life was changed. I settled down at Windhaven."

She looked down at her plate for a long time, and finally I
said, "Then you can go to him now, can't you?"

"Yes." But still she did not look up.

That evening Jo telephoned Windhaven and arranged to
be in town until noon of the next day. As it turned out, she
was to be there much longer. Next morning, at about ten
o'clock, I telephoned the gallery and asked for Dan. The girl
who answered did not want to let me speak to him. "Mr. Ford's

not well this morning, and is not taking any calls." I gave her my name and said that I must speak to him, that it was absolutely imperative, and that I would come to the gallery if she would not put him on the telephone. His voice was faint. "Grant?"

"Dan, I saw you in the street yesterday, running. I don't think you saw me. But I knew that something had happened."

"Yes. I'm through here," he said.

"What?"

"I'm through here. I can't go on."

"Dan, I've found Josephine Drew."

Silence, and then, "What, Grant?"

"Josephine Drew. I've found her. I know her well. She's coming to talk to you."

"When?"

"Right now. May I bring her?"

"She's with you? Jo Drew?"

"Outside this phone booth. We're ten minutes from you. May I bring her right now? I won't come in with her. Just she and you."

"Yes," he said, and his voice had gone almost entirely away.

And then I said, "But, Dan. There's something else. I don't want there to be any misunderstanding. She's going to marry me."

Silence.

"Dan, Dan. Are you there?"

Then two feeble words. "I'm glad."

"We'll be right there, Dan."

I came out of the telephone booth and said to Jo, "It's worse than I thought. Something drastic has happened to him. But he's ready for you." And as we got out of our taxi at the door of the gallery, I said, "But it's better that I shouldn't come in with you. I'll walk to the river and back. About forty-five minutes. Then I'll meet you here, outside. Don't hurry. I'll wait. Right?"

"All right." She pressed my hand and went up the stairs and into the door. I started walking east.

It was a mild gray day and I walked slowly to the end of Fifty-seventh Street, where there is a small, brick-paved square. I leaned on an iron railing and looked at a nurse holding four pale balloons, blue and yellow, and a single child, with four others, blue and pink. The leafless trees thrust up their awkward branches and a few sparrows hopped through them and swept away. The sparsest snowflakes drifted on the air. Something about the scene, perhaps just those balloons with their poor show of color in the general grayness, made me suddenly and acutely aware of the poverty of human experience and its pathos, and as I turned to start back to meet Jo, whose life with me, I was determined, would be rich and various, I thought again of Milly, who was so different from her. Was she, I wondered, striving all the time for what seemed to her to be "identity," a real maturity of being? Then how mistaken! Her vanity —no, it was not vanity. It was a strange inversion of egotism, in which she seemed to *absorb* the qualities of the men who bolstered it; as if, not content to bind them to her, she must acquire their *virtu* as well—the emotional aggressiveness of the fascistic Freddie; the once charming indifference to reality of the aesthete, Dan; and when she and I had had our brief affair, even some of the human tolerance that, I perhaps flatter myself, is my quality, and with that, some of my insecurity. It was very strange, this thing about Milly, as if, never "possessed" herself, she must make possession hers. Could even Josephine Drew undo the bands of that possession?

I walked slowly back, and even before I came to the gallery, I saw that the police were there, two of them blocking the door, two others with the ambulance.

Jo told me most of what had happened, but some of it I learned from Dan himself as he talked incoherently through the wire that separated us in the prison. A number of things had happened between the time that he had ordered me out of the gallery and that last day. At the beginning of the year, for example, a play had opened that caused a good deal of controversy. It was the most vigorous of all those anti-fascist plays that were coming and going, and it involved, beside a good deal of shooting, torture and murder of peculiarly violent and perverse sorts on stage. Milly and Freddie had tickets, and had assumed that Dan would have no interest in going with them, but for some reason, a rare determination to test himself, perhaps, he insisted on going, too. Milly and Freddie said that under no circumstances was that possible, that the play would completely upset him, and then that, very well, none of them would go, it was just another of those propaganda things anyway. But then Dan insisted, and finally all of them went, and in the middle of the first act he became violently ill and had to be taken out of the theater by Freddie and an usher.

He was home, in bed, for a week or more after that, and when he went back to work he found himself in such a state of nervous exhaustion that even the ordinary, routine matters of his business seemed like insuperable problems. He had reached the stage in which he had lost the power of all decision; decision, he assured me, not in matters of importance, but in the most trivial details, so that all his energies were suddenly involved in an interminable debate between pointless alternatives. A doctor decided for them that he must not try to go on, that Freddie would have to take over the gallery completely until Dan was once more able to do so. That he would never know that time again, Dan told me, he was utterly convinced; and for the first time, as he contemplated his own endless, gray, and invalided future, he resented Freddie. In a dim way, a picture of the true state of affairs was forming in his mind. Jo's visit to the gallery flooded that picture with a light that blinded him.

It was the morning on which Dan was to leave the gallery. He was going over files and accounts with Freddie. Actually, of course, Freddie was far more familiar with Dan's business than Dan was, but some obscure impulse to preserve as much of his integrity as he could muster from the ruins had prompted him to enact this fiction that Freddie needed to be instructed. They were at Dan's desk when Jo was shown in. The desk was covered with papers, and the large flat center drawer was open. The revolver which, as the owner of a gallery housing treasures, Dan was permitted to keep, lay there. He would not, of course, have calculated murder; nor would the mere presence of that weapon have been enough to bring him to it; a particular and fatal taunt was essential. That she made it was Milly's vast miscalculation.

Jo Drew had not planned to tell Dan of the way in which they had been deceived. That was damage done, she said, not to be undone. So she entered in a casual, friendly way and told Dan that she had heard that he was not well and that she hoped he would consider coming back to Windhaven. At first, Freddie was simply silent, and everything might have been all right if he had remained silent; but presently he began to bristle and bluster and finally he interrupted rudely to ask Jo to mind her own affairs.

Dan was pleased to see her. He had not, for example, told Freddie of my call or that she was on her way. Now he listened to her carefully and even pulled himself together sufficiently to show her some deference, a kind of halting gallantry that moved her. But Freddie was outraged and asked her to leave.

"May I talk to you alone?" Jo begged Dan.

"Go away, Freddie," he said.

"I will not. Your welfare is our concern, not hers. Why is she here? We have a doctor. Who sent her?"

"Get out, Freddie," Dan said, and Freddie went. He went, however, to telephone Milly, whose apartment, after all, was not six blocks away. Then, while he waited for her, he listened at the door, and he burst into that private room where they were just before Milly arrived, just as Jo did tell, as she was forced, at last, to do, of Milly's treachery and Freddie's complicity.

For when Dan and Jo were alone together, Dan slipped at once into one of his spells of despondency. She had offered him an alternative which, however attractive it may have seemed at first, was far too drastic for him to contemplate for long. He deplored his condition, he complained, he lamented; but there was, he said, no hope for him. He was best in Milly's hands.

Jo explained to him how mistaken Milly's care had been, and showed him, in as much detail as she could command, what had been done to him. To this recital he listened with lethargic sorrow, and half assented. "Perhaps," he said, "they were wrong, but they love me."

"I loved you once," she said, and then told him the rest.

Then Freddie burst in. He seized Jo and tried to force her out. He was yelling, "She's lying, Dan. A lot of lies!" But Dan picked up the revolver from his desk.

"Let her go, Freddie!"

Then Milly strode in. "Put down the gun, Dan," she said calmly. She was wearing that coat, which, under the circumstances, must in itself have been a kind of taunt.

"This woman—" Freddie began.

"Let her go!" Dan cried again, and raised the revolver.

"I don't know what lies she's told you," Milly said, "but I want Freddie to put her out, and I want you to put the gun down."

His eyes moved from Freddie to Milly, wavered, then back to Freddie. "Let her go!"

"Put the gun down, Dan," Milly said again.

"Put the gun down, Dan," Jo said then. "I haven't told any lies, but put the gun down, Dan, and come with me."

Then Milly made her error. If he was asked again, he would put it down for Jo, but he would not put it down for her. In that moment, it must have been vanity at last and vanity alone that moved her, for she started to walk easily toward Dan, saying, and saying apparently with that smiling high scorn with which I was all too familiar, "Very well, hold it if you like. It doesn't matter. You couldn't fire it, darling!"

He fired it, and, as Freddie pushed Jo aside and ran to seize the gun, Dan turned slowly toward him and fired it again.

Before the trial, I was allowed to see him only once. He pressed his forehead against that wire between us and poured out incoherent details of the shooting to me, and of the events of the weeks before, talked rapidly and desperately, in fragments, then, suddenly dispiritedly, and gradually fell silent. I had not come to hear that, and did not urge him to go on. For I had a responsibility in the disaster, since it was I who had interfered, and it was my turn now to talk rapidly and at length and with fervor, searching in him for an escape. But he did not seem to care, he did not listen.

He sat on his stiff chair and shuddered, and his stare passed through me as though I were wire, too. Then I tried to comfort him. I tried to persuade him that there are climaxes in life when to go on living is not the major value, when a man saves himself through destruction, when a man's triumph lies in his doom. But he was himself only a remnant, only a rag of a man by then, and he had really passed beyond moral assurances, as he had passed beyond salvation.

And that, except for a coda that pertains only to me, is the end of the story. Is that coda worth playing through? Does it pertain, really, at all, this last part of what happened to me? Some voice insists that it does.

Very well. But there are two questions: what happened to me in a final sense, and what happened to me immediately.

I cannot answer the first very ably, and I am not at all sure that with the onslaughts of middle age, the necessity of reading glasses and the occasional extraction of a tooth, the deterioration of pleasure, and the confusion of all public issues—I am not at all sure that I have any wish to answer. I should like to leave it at the level of generality, to say only that I did not get the girl when I was still able to have a girl, and beyond that—well, we all read the newspapers, we all know that war is our condition, that everybody gets drafted in one way or another, that there is to be no peace in our time even though no one really seems to know why there cannot be. We can only ask why people such as those in this story can allow love to become such a fatality, and remind ourselves of the poet who wrote that "There never was a war that was not inward."

I can answer the second question, the question of my immediate fate, more easily, for it involves no speculation, only the facts again. After that last unsatisfactory session with Dan, I went to Jo's hotel. A conviction bore me, the conviction of which I have spoken: that here was *my* salvation, that for me nothing yet was too late. I begged her to marry me. I held her for an hour, two hours, at a corner table in a paltry cocktail lounge, made her stay there while I told this story again, or as much of it as she did not already know. Once more I must have told it badly, for when I finished, she said, "No, I don't like it."

And she told me why not.

I left her. I fled through the lobby, ran down the steps and into the street. It was raining, and dazzled by rain and the long, bright reflections, and dazed besides, I started across the street against a light. Brakes screamed, horns blasted, and then I was like a small island around which the violent currents of traffic swept. Alone there, I was overcome by the old terror of the cliff wall. I was hanging over perilous air, and in some automatic gesture of recollection, I flung out my arms to grasp for rock as I hung there. Then the lights changed, and I limped across the rest of that street and then leaned against a building in the rain. My head was throbbing. I was shaking. Rain poured down upon me.

Always I have heard a voice asking, *who are you really?* I heard it now, and now I could answer. *You ask? I,* THE PIG, *the perfect pig, in the world I made!*

And still it was not over. Standing there in the rain in the city street, I could still wish for a chance, still, oh God, yearn for it, for another chance, even as, looking back over this whole stretch for a point at which it might have been really different, I could not see any place where another chance might ever have begun, for it all seemed to be made up of endings alone, endings and endings and endings, and no beginnings at all, never a place to start from.

OUTSTANDING BOOKS FROM SECOND CHANCE PRESS. All titles come in $16.95 cloth editions and $8.95 trade paper editions unless otherwise noted.

Bloom, Harry. TRANSVAAL EPISODE. "Fiery and admirable, with power, passion and a controlled savagery that makes it uncomfortable but fascinating reading." *London Daily Telegraph.*

Broun, Heywood Hale. A STUDIED MADNESS. "The most ruefully articulate, inside book on the American Theater in years." *John Barkham.* "A highly entertaining memoir that could be mistaken for a novel." *Milwaukee Journal.*

Conrad, Earl. GULF STREAM NORTH. "A graphic recounting of five days at sea. The crew is black, the captain white, but all are bound together in the mystique and commerce of fishing. A first class reissue." *San Diego Union.*

Crompton, Anne Elliot. THE SORCERER. A crippled Indian boy learns to control supernatural forces. "The unadorned language of folk literature; words woven together in a moody and rhythmic balance." *New York Times.*

Degenhard, William. THE REGULATORS. "This six hundred page novel to end all novels about Dan Shays will not let you down. It manages to endow the uprising known as Shays Rebellion with all the sweep of a minor epic." *New York Times.* (cloth $22.50: paper $11.95)

deJong, Dola. THE FIELD. "An overwhelming tragedy of refugees escaping Europe during World War II, this novel can tell us more about history than do books of history themselves." *St. Louis Globe Democrat.*

Goodman, Mitchell. THE END OF IT. "A classic of American literature; the single American masterpiece about the Second World War." *The Nation* "Philosophical, poetic, it says something new about war." *Norman Mailer.*

Laxness, Halldor. THE ATOM STATION. An American offer to lease an atomic base in Iceland allows this Nobel Prize winning author to serve up a black comedy peopled with Brechtian characters.

Levy, Alan. SO MANY HEROES. "Alan Levy lived through the Russian-led invasion of Czechoslovakia in 1968 and has written about it with an intimacy of detail and emotion that transcends mere journalistic reporting. A large book about a tiny nation's hope and tragedy." *Newsweek.*

Lortz, Richard. LOVERS LIVING, LOVERS DEAD. "The sort of subtle menace last evinced in Henry James' *The Turn of the Screw.* This portrait of innocence corrupted should keep a vast readership in its terrifying grasp." *San Diego Union.*

Lortz, Richard. THE VALDEPEÑAS. "The story begins with a seemingly realistic depiction of a group of vacationers summering off the coast of Spain . . . then becomes progressively surrealistic. Suspense builds to a chaotic ending making this a one-sitting, hard-to-put-down book." *Library Journal.*

O'Neal, Charles. THREE WISHES FOR JAMIE. "A humorous, sensitive love story with adventure, laughter, tears and a sprinkling of Irish folklore." *Los Angeles Times.*

Pennell, Joseph Stanley. ROME HANKS. "Such a picture of the Civil War has not heretofore been painted. A fantastic and utterly original book." *Philadelphia Inquirer.*

Salas, Floyd. TATTOO THE WICKED CROSS. "An extraordinarily evocative novel set on a California juvenile prison farm. One of the best and most important first novels published during the last ten years." *Saturday Review.*

Schorer, Mark. THE WARS OF LOVE. "A grimly powerful story of deceit and self-deception depicting the deterioration of three men and the woman who tries to dominate their lives . . . The product of a major writer." *New York Times*

Schuman, Julian. CHINA: AN UNCENSORED LOOK. "It is appropriate, timely and fortunate for those who wish to know how it was in China during the momentous years from 1948 through 1953 that the *Second Chance Press* has reprinted this book. Its time has come." *Foreign Service Journal.*

Shepard, Martin. FRITZ. The definitive biography of the founder of Gestalt Therapy. "A masterful yet loving portrait that goes far beyond biography, offering a Fritz Perls to whom few, if any, were privy." *Psychology Today.*

Singer, Loren: THE PARALLAX VIEW. "A tidy, taut and stylish thriller that functions as a political chiller as well! Breathtaking suspense." *New York Magazine.*

Stern, Richard: THE CHALEUR NETWORK "A brilliant fusing of the themes of a father's attempt to understand and exonerate his son with a plot of wartime espionage." *Richard Ellmann* "Brilliant . . . authentic . . . exciting." *Commonweal.*